Amelie's
Journey

by

Johanna Jackson

ISBN
Paperback :   978-1-80031-891-5
Ebook :   978-1-80031-890-8

www.newgeneration-publishing.com

New Generation Publishing

Dedicated to my wonderful husband, who has been my rock and best friend, during a time of change, challenge and personal growth.

Acknowledgements

My undying thanks goes to the people who have helped bring this story to life, through sharing a family story, suggesting improvements and helping with editing and fact-checking. So, my first thank you goes to Mike and Joe, who run The Crescent Post Office and Stores in Bude (keeping the family tradition going), and whose own family story helped to breathe life into this storyline. Thanks also go to my darling Niece, Samantha, my dear friend Merrenna and to Sarah, for their valuable and honest feedback. Without your input, this story would have felt very different to how it now reads. Thank you.

Finally, my thanks go to New Generation Publishing, for their advice and help in bringing this book into your hands.

Contents

Chapter 1

Losing Caden

An uncontrollable tear ran down Amelie's cheek and was immediately cooled by the gentle breeze, as it wafted across the rolling clifftops. Caden would never be forgotten by her, but as Amelie stared down into the waves crashing onto the rocks below, her reddish-brown hair blowing in the wind, she also longed to know where he was now.

Imagining she could hear her husband talking to her, Amelie felt reassured by the familiar sound of his voice, which carried towards her on the breeze, like a soft gentle whisper speaking the words, "*I will always be with you my darling...*"

Those words sounded so clear and convincing that Amelie ached to believe what she heard, just as much as her underlying faith also wanted to dismiss it. Having been taught from a young age to believe that when you're dead, you're dead, and that there is no life after this one, Amelie had come to accept that belief as the truth. Until she lost Caden. Now, her childhood teachings were being challenged by a longing to know that there *was* a life-after, because to know her Caden was still out there, somewhere, brought great comfort to Amelie.

Staring down at their beach, she remembered Caden running into the surf, then turning back to look towards her, his skin bronzed by the sun, with a glistening mop of golden hair and striking blue eyes that were always smiling. Caden always pleaded with her to join him in the surf, whilst knowing Amelie's answer was likely to be a definite 'no', followed by an exchange of casual laughter between the two of them. Caden knew of Amelie's reluctance at being in deep water only too well, although he had never fully understood it. Even when they were children, she had been afraid to venture into the water to swim, whilst he had always been the first to run into the surf. Amelie would trot alongside him, her feet staying in the shallows, her toes reassured by the firmer sand, as she laughed at him, throwing himself into the waves. Amelie had always felt slightly envious that Caden was so confident in the water.

The two of them had grown-up loving those warm summer days and had spent hours on what they had come to know as, *their beach,* and even though other people occasionally shared this particular little section, it was still *theirs*, it belonged to them and was a part of them, and as far as they were concerned, other people were just sharing their sand.

The day's heat had dropped and despite the petticoats beneath her long skirt, a chill ran through Amelie as she wrapped her shawl around herself a little tighter, wanting the comfort it offered to stay with her. It felt so unfair, they were both still so young. How could he leave her? Why didn't he want to stay?

Amelie's pain was still very raw and she had experienced so many clashing emotions since Caden had passed, that now, in this moment, as the sun began to sink towards the horizon, her sense of loss was just too much to bear. As her tears ran unchecked, Amelie's bewildered green eyes looked up at the sky and she cried out, "Why? Why did you take him?"

But, no sooner had she finished that painful cry, than a calm and gentle voice seemed to say, "*He wasn't taken*

Amelie, it was his path and his chosen end to this life."

Feeling defiant and convinced that Caden loved her too deeply to want to leave her, Amelie rejected that thought – his utter devotion to her had always been obvious – so much so, that some of the folks in their little township of Bude, were quite envious of the depth of love the young couple had shared. Whilst others had admired how their childhood friendship had blossomed into such passionate love. So popular were they, that there had been much celebration and merriment when the two of them had finally decided to marry. Everyone loved a wedding and it had seemed as though theirs was celebrated by most of the towns-people.

Both Caden and Amelie's families had been among the wealthiest in the town and because of that, between them, they had been able to hire a school-teacher. Such was their generous community nature, the two families ensured that any local children who had shown a willingness and an aptitude for learning, were also included in these classes. Which is how Caden and Amelie had come to know each other so well. They had grown up together and learnt together. Known by virtually everyone in the local community, the two families were much admired for the generous gift of learning they had shared as widely as possible. The young people of Bude had much to thank them for.

Caden had always known he would marry Amelie and he loved the fact that she was different to the other girls. Fiercely independent and strong-willed, Amelie was a true free-spirit. Caden had often joked that her reddish-brown hair and green eyes were the cause of such defiance, whenever she had found herself at odds with adult's expectations of the life a young woman should live. Amelie was adamant that she wanted a different life to

3

that which was still expected of most young women her age – many of whom had been brought up to marry, obey their husbands, have lots of babies and stay at home to support those husbands, no matter what choices he made on their behalf – Amelie had always challenged that expectation and was enthusiastic about exploring life, which was why Caden loved her so much and had felt so determined to support Amelie in *her* dreams, as much as she did him, in his. It was the 1900s after all and Amelie's own mother, who had moved to Cornwall from the higher society in London, had been very well-read, teaching her daughter everything she knew, including, that women should consider themselves as equal to men, in terms of learning abilities and ambition.

For Amelie, the need for equality was a burning desire inside her and she wanted to break the mould of generations past, and fly free, doing whatever she wanted to do. Just like Caden had, when he decided to become a volunteer lifeboatman.

Both of them had known the risks of that role only too well, but Amelie had supported his decision, in spite of her own fears that his life would be in mortal danger, every time they launched the lifeboat. But Amelie also understood and loved Caden's unshakable willingness to help others. Saving lives was how he saw it and that caring nature was one of his many endearing qualities. In her eyes, Caden had always been a real-life hero and for as long as she could remember, he had encouraged her, never dampening her spirit or zest for life. Caden had truly cared about making sure Amelie was happy. The two of them had been perfect for each other. Which is why losing him had devastated her so much.

The breeze whispered to her again, *"He was a good man Amelie and he lived a fulfilled life."*

Amelie thought back at how the whole town had mourned Caden. People had travelled from all around to honour the brave lifeboatman, who had become such an integral part of their community. He was loved by everyone and Amelie had found herself overwhelmed by offers of condolences and support, when Caden had passed. At the time, feeling unable to accept that he was gone, all Amelie had wanted to do was run away, or scream to whoever was listening *up there*, insisting that she wanted her Caden back.

Such inconsolable grief had been understandable and tangible to everyone around her, all of them very aware that just two years previously, Amelie had also lost both of her parents in a boating accident. Being a fishing community and working the often, rough waters around their jagged coastline, many families had experienced the loss of a father, brother, or cousin to the sea. Which is why they offered empathy, as well as sympathy, in their attempts to comfort the grief-stricken Amelie. Yet, despite such generous support, she had still felt completely lost without her precious Caden.

In the days that followed Caden's funeral, reflecting on the shared memories and funny stories that so many people had relayed to her, Amelie slowly realised that it was not just *she* who had lost Caden, *everyone* had lost him and each felt their own pain at his passing. The loss of one so young and the sad circumstances of his death was utterly tragic, and had affected their whole community.

The week they lost him had been during a particularly warm and sunny spell of fine weather, which had seen many visitors suddenly descending upon Bude; all aiming for the beach and keeping the Dippers very busy, as they helped the wealthier ladies change into the latest must-have bathing costumes, before tripping down to the water's edge to test the temperatures of the cool North Atlantic waters, known to the locals as the Celtic Sea. On those hot and sunny days, the water had felt so welcoming and refreshing, particularly for some of the older ladies, who dressed with almost as many clothes for bathing, as they wore when away from the beach. Dressed as they were in such heat and feeling hot enough to pass out, the ladies were always thankful of the cool water as it splashed their legs and soaked through their bathing costumes. The younger women were glad of the shorter bathing costume styles, which gave them greater freedom of movement, even once they were wet through.

On that particular day, after cooling-off in the Celtic Sea and changing back into their dry clothes, three young ladies who had become holiday friends, decided to walk a short way along the coastal path. Wanting to explore a little, they climbed up the steep slope of the downs, to investigate the popular *Compass Point,* before looking back down over Summerleaze Beach. Feeling brave and not aware of the dangers of a crumbling cliff-face, one young lady, known to her new friends as Betty, had leaned over the edge, to look down onto the beach below, but as she stepped back, the earth beneath her feet started to give way. Screaming with fear and as her new friends watched in horror, Betty had fallen as if in slow motion, causing them to also scream, as they saw Betty disappear over the edge. Whilst Betty struggled to catch hold of the plants and grasses growing from the cliff-face, the noise of their combined screams carried on the breeze, heading towards the harbour. Startled by the unexpected sound and realising someone was in trouble, three men headed off in the direction of the commotion, unaware of the situation ahead, but very well aware that the screaming meant something bad had obviously happened. Caden had been one of those men.

Having grabbed hold of a strong mass of sea-grass, Betty was clinging-on with all her strength as she desperately tried to find a foothold. Fearing for her life, as she struggled to hold-on, Betty shouted at her new friends to get help. As one of them set-off to raise the alarm, the other dropped down onto her tummy and lying back from the edge of the cliff, called out to Betty, desperately trying to encourage her to hold-on, telling her that help would soon be on its way.

As the three men hurried towards the cliff-top, they saw Betty's young friend rushing towards them, calling out to bring rope. Caden instructed the other two to continue on and ran back to fetch a rope. Finding two more of the lifeboat crew in the harbour-master's hut, he instructed them to grab hold of a large fishing net, whilst he picked up the longest rope he could see. Making their way back to the sound of the women screaming, each man worried whether they would arrive in time. The weight of the rope and netting slowed them down considerably, making the steep climb feel even more arduous.

When they arrived, a quick assessment of the situation had already been made by the first two rescuers. Caden needed to go over the top, he was younger and fitter than the others, besides which, their combined strength and weight would be invaluable in hauling both him and Betty back up the cliff. Without hesitation, Caden tied the rope around himself, whilst the others threw the fishing net halfway over the cliff edge, instructing Betty's two friends to sit on it, whilst the four men also stood on it; each of them praying their combined weight would be enough to prevent them all from being pulled over the cliff-edge. Their aim was for the net to provide something for Caden and Betty to grip onto, as they climbed back up. It was a dangerous manoeuvre which could have potentially taken them all over the edge, but experience and their combined strength convinced the men that this was the best option.

Watching Caden lowering himself over the edge had momentarily turned Betty's fear to hope, until, unable to hold her own weight, she lost grip with one hand and screamed again as she slipped to one side. Caden quickly lowered himself to the left of Betty and knowing he was within arms-reach of her, in an unplanned, automatic reaction, he swung himself across and grabbed hold of Betty around her waist, yanking her into him with his right arm, as he held onto the rope with his left. The men, holding onto the rope at the top, strained against the sudden force and leant backwards to add more power to their stance. A crying and relieved Betty instinctively wrapped her arms around Caden, as awkwardly, they crashed back against the cliff-face. Trying to protect the young woman he had rescued, Caden somehow managed to put himself between Betty and the cliff, just as his head hit it with a sickening thud. Blood immediately trickled from a gash just above his ear. Betty was still clinging onto Caden, terrified he would drop her after seeing the blood seeping from his head-wound. The men above, immediately began heaving with all their might, calling out to them both to hold-on tight. Caden was thankful of their strength, as his own began to wane and he battled to hold onto both Betty, and the rope. Caden was determined to keep her safe and as they reached the fishing net, he instructed Betty to grab onto it.

Unsure of the strength of the seemingly fine netting and not knowing if it would take her weight, instinctively, Betty grabbed hold of it, thankful of the sense of safety it offered. Gripping each handful of net tightly, Caden helped push her up and as she reached the top, Betty was unceremoniously pulled over the edge by two of the men.

Crying with relief, Betty's friends reached out to comfort her. Caden, his face and neck now covered in blood, collapsed onto the grass as he reached topside. He was exhausted and his wound was bleeding profusely. Concerned at the amount of blood he was losing and having already noted that although Betty was shaken, she was surprisingly, unhurt, the men promptly tended to Caden.

Betty, still distraught and exhausted from her fall, was overwhelmed at surviving her close encounter with death, and feeling utterly grateful to her heroes, she thanked them all profusely, most especially, Caden. As was typical of his character, Caden had just nodded his acceptance of Betty's gratitude and suggested in future, that she and her friends stay away from the unsafe cliff-edge. Betty agreed and leaning on her friends, the three of them gingerly made their way back down to the house, where Betty's family were staying.

It had taken Caden a good few minutes to recover well enough to stand, before he too was helped back down the steep coastal path, by his fellow lifeboat crew, who between them, also carried the rope and fishing-net, having retrieved them from the broken cliff edge.

By the time Amelie finally saw Caden, his face, neck and chest were completely covered in blood and the rag that had been given to him to stem the blood-flow was soaked through. The doctor was sent for, as Caden was brought inside and helped up to their bedroom. The shock of his injury and subsequent blood loss, had affected Caden's body temperature and as a sudden coldness hit him, he passed out.

The doctor arrived quickly and amid instructions to fetch warm water and clean rags, he tended to Caden, informing them all that the wound needed to be cleaned and stitched. Amelie was relieved when the doctor took control and watched as he set to work, stemming the bleed and stitching the wound closed. Unable to bear watching the needle being pushed through Caden's skin, Amelie had looked away, whilst the men held Caden's shoulders down and kept his head very still in case he came to. Just as the doctor tied off the last stitch, Caden opened his eyes. Feeling weak from the blood loss, he had no energy to argue and no option other than to obey the doctor, when instructed to remain where he was and rest.

The crewmen had joked about scars making Caden less handsome and finally giving them all a chance with the ladies, but secretly, they were all concerned that the injury was likely to be worse than it looked. Being aware of Amelie's worried face, they tried to keep the mood as upbeat as possible and thankfully, their humour seemed to work, taking the sting out of the seriousness of the situation, temporarily reassuring Amelie that Caden was strong and would be fine.

It seemed such an age before the men and the doctor finally left them alone, with instructions for Amelie to send a message if there was any further dizziness, sickness, or blood loss. Caden had tried to reassure them all that he was feeling a bit better, but it wasn't until he had been able to drink a cup of freshly-brewed tea, that a relieved Amelie would believe he was going to be fine. She had even laughed as Caden joked that his new scar would be a good talking point at the pub.

As the raw memories flooded back into her mind, Amelie remembered preparing a late supper and taking it to Caden in bed, telling him not to worry and that yes, she knew of the dangers of the crumbling cliffs, and yes, she would stay away from them. Later, as they both drifted towards sleep, Caden had told Amelie he loved her very much.

The night passed without incident and as the dawn chorus erupted, Amelie had awoken, immediately feeling shocked that they had both slept for so long. Remembering the loving words Caden had whispered to her the night before, Amelie glanced across at him and admired her sleeping husband, who looked so handsome, and peaceful. Gently sliding out of bed, so as not to disturb him, she made her way downstairs to re-stoke the fire and make them both some tea. Carefully carrying the cups and saucers back upstairs, not wanting to spill anything on their new bedroom rug, Amelie had set the cups down on Caden's side of the bed, before tenderly leaning over to kiss his lips...

"Nooooo!"

A blood-curdling scream of disbelief echoed throughout their small house, as Amelie collapsed against the bed, her shock evident on her face. Caden's lips were icy-cold and as she touched his cheek, realisation immediately dawned that her beloved Caden was gone and would no longer feel the warmth of her touch, or the depth of her love.

The pain had shot through her like an arrow, wounding every organ in its path, before causing her heart to shatter into a million pieces.

Neighbours, having heard Amelie's screams, had banged on the door downstairs, calling out to ask if everything was alright, before they somehow managed to force their way in. Rushing upstairs, they had found the heartbroken and sobbing Amelie, lying across Caden's lifeless body, holding his head in her arms, as she cried into his hair, utterly distraught that the love of her life was now gone from her forever.

The kindness of Amelie's neighbours poured into the room as they took over, one sending for the doctor to confirm Caden's death, whilst two others took care of Amelie.

The week following Caden's death passed by in a haze, with a constant stream of well-meaning people dropping by, offering condolences and insisting on helping with Caden's funeral. But no amount of consolation could take Amelie's pain away and it seemed there was nothing anyone could do to help. Amelie's sense of loss was overwhelming and as the weeks rolled into months, two years passed by in the blink of an eye.

Now, stood on top of the cliff, she was able to think back with fondness at the times they had shared on their beach. But even now, despite that fondness, the pain still felt raw. Watching as the sun began to set, Amelie marvelled as the sky turned into a mass of warm pinks, oranges and yellows, burning across the horizon and delaying the evening darkness. It was one of the most beautiful sunsets Amelie had seen in a very long time and as she looked up in awe at the stunning skies above her head, momentarily, her soul felt uplifted. But as the sun began its final descent below the horizon, that temporary sparkle diminished with it and Amelie's zest for life dulled again, as she turned to walk back home, alone. Caden had been the greatest joy in her life and now, without him, nothing would ever be the same again.

* * * * * * *

Over the past two years, Caden had watched his beautiful Amelie from a place that she could not see. The sunset had always been their favourite time, but as he watched her this evening, he was saddened that her grief prevented her from moving forwards. Wanting to re-energise his beautiful and loving wife, Caden's only regret at leaving his earthly life so soon, was seeing how much his loss was affecting Amelie. It was unbearable to him. Amelie's life was continuing, of that he was grateful, but her essence was numbed by her grief and Caden knew he had to help find a way to re-ignite that burning fire in her belly.

Seeking out a higher counsel, Caden learned that whilst he could leave a sign to show he was around Amelie, it was not for him to decide how her life should progress. This was Amelie's life and how she lived, had to be her choice. Whilst free will is given to every human spirit when their new life begins, like Caden, Amelie's life would follow the path she has chosen, using her own free will. Caden knew only too well, exactly how free Amelie's spirit had been, but he now felt frustrated that it was not shining as brightly as it had, when he had shared her life. What sign could he give her?

* * * * * * *

Chapter 2

Friendship

Women working for a living was still frowned upon in many households, but with no man to support her and being the free-spirit she was, Amelie needed to work, as much as she needed the air to breathe and so, making her own way in life, she had started up a town newsletter after Caden died. The newsletter quickly became very popular and seemed like a good way to fill her time.

Not wanting to be beholden to anyone, the rebel instincts Amelie had always had, still rumbled deep within her, but finally, she had found something to capture her interest and satisfy her craving for being different to other women. The newsletter soon grew in size, as did the number of advertisers who clamoured to be included and with the profit she made from each page printed, Amelie was able to improve her stock of printing equipment from early-on. It was a dream come true and the newsletter meant everything to her.

"Amelie!" A deep throated voice shouted through the open doorway, "Are you there? Is it fine to come in?" Feeling a little startled by the unexpected voice calling out, Amelie walked through to her workshop front-door, only to be greeted by Dylan, who was waiting on the doormat, aware of his very muddy boots. Dylan had been Caden's only other best-friend and he had looked in on her at least twice a week since Caden had passed. The two men had been childhood friends and grown up with Amelie in their midst. In fact, Dylan had always held a soft spot for Amelie, but knowing Amelie's affections lay with Caden, he had stood back over the years.

It hadn't stopped Dylan caring for her though and as the years had passed, so his feelings for Amelie had deepened and he had felt compelled to tell Caden. Caden was shocked, but actually really good about it, he understood the attraction of course, but he also valued Dylan's honesty, telling him he was a good friend and how only the best of men would be brave enough to share their feelings in the way Dylan had. Dylan had felt relieved to finally tell Caden, but he had been honourable and since Caden's passing, had never once tried to take things further with Amelie.

Amelie had always sensed that Dylan felt something stronger than friendship for her, but to be fair to him, as far as she was concerned, Dylan had never once spoken out of turn, or made any attempt to steal her away from his best friend. No. Dylan had integrity and was a very decent man, who worked hard on a farm just outside of Bude, where he was greatly respected by his local community of Marhamchurch. The village was small, little more than a hamlet really, where everyone knew everyone, which suited him just fine. Dylan drew comfort from living in such a close community and valued the fact that whilst everyone knew each other's business, they also had each other's backs and would step-in to help whenever needed. Which is also why Dylan had not been surprised by the turnout for Caden's funeral, because to him, that's what their respective communities did.

"Hello Dylan, how are you?" Amelie was curious as to why Dylan had turned up in the middle of the day, when he would normally be working.

"I'm great thanks Amelie, always better for seeing you." Dylan couldn't resist slipping in a confirmation to

Amelie of how much he valued seeing her, "Old man Jake had to go to the doc's, he cut his hand pretty bad and needs a couple of stitches."

Dylan had brought the land-owner turned farmer into Bude because the only doctor in Marhamchurch was away up country, visiting his sister, Mary, who had married an emmet (tourist) and moved to Hampshire. Apparently, their first baby was due any day and whilst she trusted her local midwife, she had wanted her doctor-brother to be there in case of problems. Dylan hadn't really been that interested in the explanation provided by the Marhamchurch doctor's housekeeper, but only because he was concerned for old Jake and knew his hand needed urgent attention. Thankfully, the new tractor, which had arrived two days ago, was perfect for getting Jake over to Bude fairly quickly, and could manage a short-cut across the fields just as easily as any horse. With old Jake unable to ride on horse-back, Dylan was over the moon to be given permission to drive them on the new tractor. Old Jake had already decided it would likely be Dylan using the tractor anyway, so he wasn't worried about handing over the controls and besides, they'd both been messing about with it the previous day, so Jake knew Dylan could handle it. The two men were as keen as each other to put their new machine to the test and both of them enjoyed the shouts and cheers they received en-route, from all the interested locals. Dylan dropped old Jake off at the doctor's house and drove down to Amelie's workshop, in the hope she would be there.

Roughly brushing down his messy dark hair with his fingers, so that it looked as tidy as he could make it, Dylan was feeling really excited, he wanted to show off the new tractor and tell Amelie that HE was the official driver.

Amelie could see that Dylan was bursting about

something and as she accepted his kiss on her cheek, she chuckled at the obvious excitement he exuded. For Dylan, it was lovely to see Amelie laugh again and he said so, which did cause her to briefly pause, before asking what it was that had him bouncing off the walls with excitement. Taking Amelie's hand, Dylan said to follow him outside.

"Well then, so that's the new tractor Jake's been so proud of telling everyone about. Goodness, it's amazing Dylan. Shall we have a closer look?" Amelie was intrigued and thought what an interesting piece it would make, for the latest edition of her newsletter.

As the two of them walked towards the new tractor, a group of townsfolk had also crossed the street to see what this new-fangled contraption was. Everyone was understandably excited, it being the first powered, mechanical farm equipment they had ever seen in the flesh. It was no wonder they were also intrigued.

Dylan offered Amelie his hand so she could step-up onto the tractor and sit in the driving seat. It was amazing and she felt very special to be one of the first people to sit on such an incredible machine. As Amelie smiled at Dylan, he beamed back at her, absolutely thrilled that finally, she was smiling at him, without either of them feeling guilty about Caden.

Dylan answered everyone's questions and gave Amelie enough information to write an article about the tractor. Deciding that including a picture alongside the article would make the piece more interesting, Amelie ran back inside her workshop to retrieve her very precious camera, which had been very generously donated to her by the family of the late Arthur Mills MP.

This was a proud moment for Dylan and as he sat upon the tractor, the locals watched and cheered, whilst Amelie took the photograph.

"Amelie, this is such a special moment." Dylan was a bit misty-eyed, "To have my photograph taken and be included in your newsletter, well, old Jake, will be sorry he cut his hand and missed out on this, that's for sure."

Dylan was prouder than he had ever been, this was indeed a precious moment, made all the more special, because Amelie was smiling again and that smile was being directed *at him*. Dylan's heart lifted and he silently thanked old Jake for cutting his hand and then allowing him to drive the tractor.

"You'll be famous yet, Dylan Mackay." Amelie beamed at Dylan, happy to have something really exciting to write about. "Come on inside and have some tea, while I process this photograph. You'll get to see what it looks like before Jake is ready to go home. I'm sure he and the doc will be chatting for a good while up at Tremethyk, seeing as it's unlikely Jake will be using that hand for the rest of the day." Dylan was more than happy to accept Amelie's invitation as he jumped down from the tractor to follow her inside. Sharing a pot of tea with Amelie was always a welcome invitation.

As Dylan enjoyed an hour of Amelie's company, he became all the more comfortable sitting beside her kitchen fire and once again, he secretly imagined becoming Amelie's husband. Yes, he could see himself in that role and knew he loved her enough for the both of them. Life would be perfect for Dylan, if Amelie were to agree to marry him. Caden had been gone for two years now and so it was time for her to move on. Dylan's imagination was flying high, along with his excitement at the new tractor sitting outside.

Amelie, on the other hand, was thinking something completely different. The sight of the tractor had piqued her already rapidly growing interest in the fast-developing world they were now living in. Amelie had already decided that she needed a bit more in her life than settling in Bude and was itching to try something new and different. It was true, Amelie needed something else to help heal the wounds of losing Caden. As Dylan chatted happily about his week on the farm, so Amelie's mind drifted to the beach and what lay across the other side of the Atlantic Ocean.

America, the land of hope and glory. A land full of promise. A land which beckoned both the young and those wanting a fresh new start at life, an exciting new future!

The thought of visiting another country excited Amelie and having heard from Archie Jewell's wife Bessie, about the beautiful ship that was soon to be making its maiden voyage, she wondered if a new future could possibly lay across the ocean for her too.

It was both receiving the letter from Bessie about her Archie having gained a lookout position onboard the Titanic and seeing an advert in the window of Hawkins Shipping Company, for tickets on the White Star Line's newest ship, RMS Titanic, that had sown a seed in Amelie's mind. Listening to Dylan talking excitedly of farming and tractors, she knew that her future needed to be very different to that of her dearest friend. Amelie definitely needed something more exciting.

Bidding Dylan goodbye as he drove the tractor back up to the doctor's house, Amelie wondered how she should break the news to him, that she was thinking of buying a ticket for RMS Titanic. Knowing how he felt about her, Amelie realised that Dylan would be devastated if she were to leave Bude, but this was *her* life and without Caden, she needed to do something that would totally thrill her and re-ignite that long-ago flame, which now smouldered inside her soul. Amelie loved Dylan dearly, but only as a friend and she needed to do this alone, for herself, even though it meant selling everything she had, to buy the ticket that would take her to an exciting new life in America.

As Amelie prepared the article about the new tractor, she imagined working for a newspaper in New York. Having read many stories from the newspapers that Bude's visitors brought down from London, Amelie's mind was racing, full of ideas and fantasies of a possible new life. An American life. In her mind, the decision was already made and Amelie knew, no matter what, she had to find enough money to buy a ticket.

Amelie decided to tell Dylan of her plans, once she had already purchased a ticket. There was no point in telling him sooner, because she knew he would try his utmost to dissuade her and convince her that her life belonged in Bude. Feeling a little guilty that she would be telling him and then leaving the very next day, Amelie knew in her heart of hearts, it was kinder to them both. Yes, Dylan would miss her and she would miss him too, but she would promise to write to him regularly, and she intended to keep that promise.

The next few months were busy for Amelie, as she quietly sold off her possessions and found someone willing to buy her newsletter business from her, having gleaned enough advertising to make it an attractive venture for the new owner. Amelie winced at the thought of selling to a buyer from up-country and she already knew that piece of news would not go down well with Dylan either. The printing equipment she had previously invested in, was an added bonus, because it meant her little business was already modern and could fetch a good price. Negotiations took place in a shroud of secrecy, it was important for Amelie not to let any knowledge of her leaving, leak out to Dylan just yet. With Amelie's parents and Caden now gone, and being an only child, she had nothing more to hold her back. This was her time and she hoped that Caden would approve, even if Dylan didn't.

* * * * * * *

Caden did approve and watched over her as Amelie's plans came together. The sign he had provided, with the prompted letter from Bessie, that had conveniently advised Amelie of the Titanic's maiden voyage, had worked out perfectly. Caden was happy to see her flame burning brighter with every day that passed. Amelie was off on an adventure of a lifetime and could choose her own new life, once she settled in America.

* * * * * * *

Chapter 3

RMS Titanic

Times were changing and Amelie was excited, tomorrow was her big day. The new owner of her local newsletter would be collecting the keys from her and following a handover of all documents, plus instructions, she would be travelling to Southampton, to sail on the most beautiful ship in the world. It would be an adventure like no other and, as New York and its newspaper industry beckoned, so Amelie's spirits lifted.

Telling Dylan had been the only stain on her adventure copybook. Realising his dreams had been shattered with the news that Amelie was leaving England, she had expected that Dylan would take it hard, but Amelie had not quite prepared herself for just how difficult it would be to actually tell him, or how hurt she would also feel, at seeing him so distraught. They had agreed to say goodbye in Bude, but then Dylan had changed his mind and insisted on accompanying her to Southampton, to ensure she reached the ship with no problems and to help her with her luggage. Despite her protestations, Dylan insisted he wanted to do this, saying Caden would want him to. In truth, it was also his way of seeing her for as long as possible, before the ship set sail. Understanding his explanation, Amelie graciously accepted Dylan's kind offer and arranged for him to meet her after the business formalities were completed. The railways network and timetable would drive their schedule and they would need to make at least two changes of train, so Amelie decided to arrange an overnight sleeper carriage for them both on the train. Amelie wanted to ensure she arrived feeling bright and chirpy, with plenty of time for boarding the Titanic; there was no way she wanted to start this adventure feeling tired from the train journey.

As the moment arrived for Amelie to board the ship, Dylan hugged Amelie fully, kissing her on both cheeks and with tears filling his eyes, reluctantly, he let her go. Convinced that he would never see her again and despite her promises to write, Dylan expected Amelie to be so taken-up with her exciting adventure, that he didn't really believe he would ever receive the promised letters. Amelie tried hard to convince him, but she also recognised and understood his fears, and thanked him for being so considerate of her new life, but more so, for being such a good friend to Caden. Amelie told Dylan she was certain that Caden would be forever grateful for his watchful eye over her; never could a person wish for a better friend and with that truthful compliment, Amelie planted a kiss on Dylan's lips and walked up the boardwalk to second class.

As the object of his unrequited love disappeared from view, Dylan stood for the longest time, heart-broken and bereft, tears now streaming down his face, his beloved Amelie was gone and he would never see her again. The reality hit him hard and Dylan finally accepted that, despite all of his hopes, dreams and wishes, Amelie would never be his.

Taking the Ship's Steward's offered hand as she reached the top of the wooden walkway and stepping down onto the deck, not in her wildest dreams had Amelie imagined she would ever be doing this. It had really only been made possible, thanks to the sale of her business, all of her possessions and the generosity of young Betty's wealthy parents. On hearing of Caden's passing and feeling so thankful that he had saved their daughter's life, they were terribly shocked and saddened that he had lost his own. Money was all they had to offer to afford Amelie some comfort and help, and so they had transferred a very large sum to her, in commemoration of Caden's brave and selfless act. Betty was their world and to still have her with them, meant everything. This additional money had meant that Amelie did not need to worry when paying for her ticket for the White Star Line's famous ship, or how she would live when she first arrived in New York.

However, she would find that as a woman travelling alone, there would be several *interesting* conversations that she would need to deal with. Some of her fellow passengers would exclaim and be shocked at her travelling unaccompanied. Whilst others would be impressed by her spirit and gutsy determination to carve out a future for herself, despite being widowed at such a young age. Respectable? Yes, she was, but still, she was also a lone woman during a time of great change in modern society. Life onboard RMS Titanic would be so very different to Amelie's life in Bude and she felt excited by the challenge of it, as she stood at the railing looking down over the dock-side, desperately searching for sight of Dylan's dark hair. Amelie thought for one moment that she had spotted him and tried to call out, but of course, he could not hear her small voice amongst the noise of the ship, let alone the crowds, who were already gathered to wave-off the magnificent Titanic on her maiden voyage. Likewise, as Dylan searched the faces at the railings, he hoped to find Amelie there, but she was too far away, too high up and all he could do was hope she could see him. The two of them had agreed to wave red handkerchiefs to help spot each other, but it seemed like dozens of others had the same thought. So, Amelie just waved and smiled, along with everyone else, hoping Dylan could see her. With tears streaming down his face, Dylan waved as hard as he could, disappointed that he could not spot Amelie, but hopeful that she could see him, before finally leaving to walk back to the station. There was no rush for him, all that waited back home was emptiness and a new tractor.

Amelie's smile broadened as she made herself comfortable in her shared cabin, feeling thankful that her travelling companion seemed not to have arrived. Rumours onboard would later be confirmed that several hundred people did not take up their places. The exact reasons were not known for the majority, but it was reported that many passengers had been forced to cancel travel-plans due to the national coal-strike. Knowing her own excitement at finally being onboard, Amelie could only begin to imagine how disappointed those travellers were, knowing they would miss this fantastic voyage.

Feeling quite happy to have her cabin to herself, Amelie began unpacking her bags and making herself at home. Humming as she unpacked and thinking about Caden, Amelie wished he was with her and said as much out loud; she was sure he whispered back to her, *"I am, my darling..."*

As Amelie explored and experienced life onboard the Titanic, it was the most exciting and totally thrilling time for her. People-watching became an instant and enjoyable habit; Amelie loved to see all the different dresses worn by the middle-class ladies, as they strolled along the promenade deck. Although, watching the facial expressions and over-heard comments from several small groups, proved to be quite the eye-opener at how some people behaved towards their fellow passengers. Society was a funny thing, Amelie decided, noting how it seemed that some passengers behaved in an appropriate manner, whilst others seemed to want to rebel against what was considered 'appropriate'. Thankfully, those *were* in the minority and Amelie managed to look past them, whilst feeling both joyous and overwhelmed with delight at this extraordinary occasion.

Wearing her warmest coat and felt hat, Amelie was also thankful of her scarf and gloves, the weather was cold, but she was determined to stand out on the ship's deck, as they arrived in Cork Harbour. Being on-deck was definitely chilly, but the whole experience of taking onboard more passengers was utterly thrilling and Amelie watched with excited anticipation, as walkways were lowered to allow them to board from the small tenders, which, between them, were carrying an additional one hundred and twenty-three Queenstown passengers. Feeling in awe of the precision with which the boarding operation took place, without thinking, Amelie voiced her thoughts. The young man stood alongside her, agreed.

"Yes, it is absolutely amazing, isn't it!"

Alfie's British accent was unmistakable, although there was a slight American twang to some of his pronunciations. Introducing himself, Alfie explained that he had been visiting his sick father in London and was on his way back to America far earlier than expected, because his darling wife – who was back home in New York – had gone into labour very early and just delivered their first child, a son, whom they were planning to call William George, after his father. Alfie was touched at Amelie's concern for his father's health and reassured her that he was expected to make a full recovery, but that it would be a slow process and require more rest.

Something his father was not used to, being quite an active man.

Amelie warmed to Alfie right away and remarked upon how his name was quite similar to her friend Bessie's husband, Archie, who was one of the look-outs on RMS Titanic, to which Alfie immediately replied saying he felt honoured to be likened to a friend of hers. Amelie was thankful of chatting to a friendly and like-minded individual, and felt grateful that Alfie did not let the fact that she was clearly travelling alone, stop him from speaking to her. After all, usual society convention would expect that she should have a travelling companion. Of course, Amelie's reason for her journey required a solo passage on this occasion, which Alfie was yet to be informed about and yet he still did not judge her.

The two of them watched the whole of the boarding process, fascinated by the speed and accuracy of the tender crews, as they ensured all passengers were safely aboard. With the boarding completed in record time, it wouldn't be long before they were off again and beginning the longest part of the voyage. Feeling chilled by the cool breeze, Alfie suggested they return inside and have some hot chocolate to warm themselves up. Enjoying each other's company and with nothing else to occupy their time, Amelie and Alfie decided to lunch together and whilst chatting, Amelie found herself talking about losing Caden, starting the newsletter business and her plans to try and get work with a large newspaper, once they reached New York.

As luck would have it, Alfie knew a reporter at the New York Times and offered to introduce Amelie, if she so wished.

If she so wished… Amelie laughed and said it would be the answer to her prayers as she thanked Alfie for his very generous offer. Maybe this exciting new life would turn out well for her after all. Making plans to meet again at dinner, Amelie and Alfie parted company after lunch. After all the excitement of the past twenty-four hours, Amelie decided she needed to return to her cabin to rest, before freshening-up for the evening entertainment and the more formal dinner. The past few weeks of excitement and anticipation, along with all the travelling by train, had quite taken it out of Amelie and she appreciated the quiet peace that her cabin afforded. Alfie, being an active man, decided he didn't need to rest and said he would hunt out the onboard gymnasium.

It was clear to Amelie that Alfie was a man who looked after himself and even though she would never say so, he was quite dashing, in a rugged kind of way and very masculine, so she was not surprised to hear he was interested in rowing machines and the like; although she suspected she might not be so lucky as to gain access to the Gymnasium onboard, having heard it was for First Class passengers only, not that exercising appealed to her right now.

Amelie had not been in her cabin long when she was startled by a rapturous knocking on the door. Waiting patiently on the other side was the nominated steward for her cabin, who introduced himself as Robert and politely apologised for disturbing her, whilst asking if she would mind another passenger joining her cabin? Robert explained that this passenger's companion had come down with a sudden bout of sickness, making their cabin quite unsuitable for sharing and so, as Amelie's fellow passenger had not turned up, this would be the best solution for the unexpected situation.

Amelie realised it would be churlish to refuse and so she accepted, graciously, and welcomed Ruby-Jane Carter to her cabin. The two young women hit it off immediately, their first observations being how similar their hair colour was, although Ruby's eyes were blue. Much to their joint delight, they found each other's company an absolute blessing, rather than the daunting prospect it had at first seemed. Taking afternoon tea together, they talked about what had brought each of them to the Titanic and what America held for them. It turned out that Ruby-Jane was a travelling companion to a wealthy lady, whose ample accommodation included a bed for her young assistant. However, the lady in question, had met a gentleman friend in London, who decided to return to America with her and had also booked a cabin in first class. Seeing how in-love her mistress was, Ruby-Jane had realised she would likely appreciate more privacy and suggested they feign a bout of sickness, to see if another cabin was available. Ruby-Jane hadn't minded at all, she was very happy for her mistress, whom she said, was an absolute delight to work for and always extremely generous towards Ruby-Jane.

Feeling equally grateful to Amelie for agreeing to share her cabin, Ruby-Jane insisted on re-paying such kindness when they reached New York; offering Amelie the spare room in her own apartment – which belonged to her mistress, but was generously provided as part of her job – just to help Amelie get started in her new life. Amelie could not quite believe such good luck and thanked her lucky stars for the opportunities that both Alfie and now Ruby-Jane were offering.

Ruby-Jane joined Amelie and Alfie for dinner. The three new friends made a jolly table for their fellow diners, who enjoyed the light-hearted banter and laughter that seemed to be never-ending across their table. The evening could not have been more perfect.

The next few days were another welcome delight and for the first time in a long time, Amelie hardly thought about Caden, or Dylan. Instead, she and Ruby-Jane had fun, meeting new people and joining in with some of the deck-games played by their fellow passengers. It was exactly the tonic that Amelie needed and finding two new friends before she had even landed, made the voyage all the more fun and exciting. Each evening of dining was a special occasion and despite a few raised eyebrows during particularly raucous parts of the conversation, everyone who was sat around their table enjoyed each evening as much as the previous one.

It was quite late by the time the ladies bade goodnight to Alfie and returned to their cabins. Alfie, feeling in need of some quiet time before retiring for the night, said he was going out on deck to enjoy the cool night air. He had only been on deck for about ten minutes when he heard shouting and a lot of commotion from several crew members. The next thing he heard was a loud grinding sound and as he rounded the deck, he saw a massive iceberg just feet from the railing and immediately realised that the ship had obviously struck the iceberg.

"Oh, my God, what's happened... surely not!" Feeling shocked and seeing how panicked the crew-members were, Alfie quickly realised the implications of the collision and his first thought was to warn his new friends, Amelie and Ruby-Jane. Running back inside, Alfie struggled to remember their cabin number. On reaching the second-class corridor, he began calling their names, loudly, whilst also banging on doors as he went, hoping to wake everyone, to give them time to prepare for an evacuation. Hearing a commotion in the corridor outside, Amelie opened the door, only to see Alfie running towards her, shouting to get Ruby-Jane and get up on deck. Hearing the urgency in his voice, Amelie questioned what on earth was wrong, Alfie just replied with, "Iceberg, we've hit an iceberg!"

Grabbing Amelie's arm, who in turn grabbed Ruby-Jane, the three of them battled through the passengers who were beginning to emerge from their cabins. Alfie knew they had to get up top, he had seen how many lifeboats there were and he knew there were not enough for all of the passengers onboard. Alfie was a chief motor engineer now, but in his past life, back in England, before he met his wealthy American wife, he had managed a tug-boat on the Thames.

Reaching the deck, proved relatively easy, but once they were there, it was chaos, people were already on deck, milling around, panic-stricken. It wasn't clear if the order to abandon ship had been given, but the lifeboats were being filled anyway. The trouble was, because the crew and officers were not trained in managing such a crisis, many of the boats were dropped into the water half-full. As people were battling to get into a lifeboat, the screams and shouting became more urgent and deafening. Alfie pushed his friends forward, shouting, "Women and children first!"

Calling out instructions at the officers managing the closest lifeboat to them, feeling disturbed by the disorganisation, Alfie tried to take command of the crowd instead, who were now surging towards the boat he was pushing Amelie and Ruby-Jane into. Seeing them being pulled-in by the officer in charge of that particular lifeboat, Alfie turned around to help the other women and children, now being shoved from behind. Shocked at how some men were pushing their way forwards, disregarding the etiquette of 'women and children first', Alfie tried unsuccessfully to push them back, only to see two small children crying; having become separated from their Guardian, they were now in danger of being crushed in the panic. Alfie jumped down and pushing people aside, he grabbed both the boy and girl in each arm, noting they couldn't be more than five or six years of age. Thankful of their slim frames, he jostled his way back through the surging crowd and passed the children to the Officer in charge of Amelie's lifeboat, who grabbed at them and virtually threw them into the boat. Amelie and Ruby-Jane gathered them up and spotting Alfie again, began screaming at him to get in the boat, but he disappeared. A man of integrity and honour, with his own wife and new-born son flashing into his head, Alfie continued to help lift women and children into whichever boat he could reach. Again, and again, Alfie turned away from the lifeboats, having given a place to someone else each time, rescuing as many people as he could.

As Amelie's and Ruby-Jane's boat was lowered into the water, the two women screamed out his name one more time, "Alfie!"

But Alfie couldn't hear them and as Titanic began to sink, the noise of it going down was horrendous, the stern was being lifted high into the air and people were falling along the decking, slipping out of each other's arms as gravity took over. Alfie managed to throw himself overboard, but the water temperature was freezing, far too cold for any human to survive for long. Alfie was fit and strong, and had long been used to cold water, but even for him it felt too cold, and as he tried to swim to the nearest lifeboat, it became more and more difficult for him to breathe. Alfie passed-out just as several hands reached out to try and haul him in. The women in the boat were not strong enough to pull the now dead-weight of Alfie and his waterlogged clothing into the boat. Crying as they fought hard to pull him out of the icy sea, from somewhere below the water, an unknown strength seemed to push Alfie up just enough for them to scrabble at him, catching hold of his clothes as they pulled him into the boat. Relief and gratitude filled the hearts of the women who had battled to save him, although they had no idea how they had suddenly managed to find enough strength to pull him aboard.

* * * * * * *

Caden had seen Alfie's own efforts to save his beloved Amelie, along with all the other women and children he had saved, and knowing Alfie's own new-born son awaited him, Caden decided to intervene. As energy was given, Caden used it to push Alfie up out of the water, so the women could pull him into the lifeboat.

* * * * * * *

Hundreds of souls were lost that night, so many more than should have been. The lifeboats were not filled to capacity and without other ships being close enough, hundreds of passengers died in the freezing waters, whilst others still remained trapped onboard Titanic. The unsinkable ship, which now lay on the sand at the bottom of the sea, was far too deep for anyone to escape from and swim to the surface. It was a devastating night and whilst some of the lifeboats returned to search for survivors, very few were found. Those who did survive, were never the same again, their lives understandably changed forever.

Chapter 4

Consequences

Everyone in the lifeboats was shocked, frozen to the bone by the cold and silenced by the utter disbelief at what they had just experienced. Archie Jewell, the lookout from Bude, had finished his duty shift and been back in his bunk when they hit the iceberg, but somehow, he had made it to lifeboat seven. Like so many others, that lifeboat only saved twenty-eight, when the capacity was for sixty-five. As the boats all drifted in the icy waters, none of them knew where they were. It was dark and dense fog made it even more difficult to see. Some of the lifeboats tried to group together, several managed it, whilst others were lost in the fog. It was around two hours later that the British Liner, RMS Carpathia, loomed into view, its lights and horn bringing hope and relief to the shocked and now frozen survivors. Many had not been dressed for such cold weather and the cold bit into their skin. Amelie and Ruby-Jane hugged each other and the two young children even closer to them, desperately trying to keep them warm. At the sound of the Carpathia's crew shouting to survivors, relief washed over every person in those lifeboats, as they gratefully watched their rescuers heading towards them.

It was a scene that no-one would ever forget, nor wish to repeat. Hundreds of frozen bodies were floating on the surface, making use of the oars difficult, without bashing into them. Even though those poor passengers were now dead, nobody wanted to hit them with oars.

Some survivors leaned over to gently pull and push the bodies away, as their boats slowly moved forwards, towards RMS Carpathia.

The Carpathia's Captain and Crew could not believe what they were seeing. Amongst the broken pieces of the iceberg, the sea was littered with human bodies. Every single crew member was affected, each of them utterly shocked at what they were witnessing, whilst grappling to pull survivors aboard. As more and more people came onboard, blankets and hot drinks began being passed around. People were thankful, but mostly silenced by the knowledge that so many lives were lost, whilst theirs had been saved. A great many men left aboard Titanic had given their places to save their families, which meant many of the survivors were women and children. It seemed as if a whole generation of men had been lost. No-one would ever forget the horror of that night.

Amelie could feel their pain, having lost her own beloved Caden, but for Ruby-Jane, this was her first experience of death and she began to shake uncontrollably, as sobs wracked her body. Holding each other and the children close, seemed the only comfort afforded the two women, as they finally sat on the deck of their rescuers ship. The children were trembling, freezing cold and scared, both were in shock, asking what had happened to their governess and parents, whilst simultaneously clinging to Amelie and Ruby-Jane, afraid to let them go. When the last people they could find were aboard, the Carpathia set off for New York, not knowing their journey was going to be made all the more difficult by the fog and storms that lie ahead. The wireless operators were kept busy all night, sending messages ahead to New York and back to England. Names were being gathered, but it was obvious even then, that hundreds of souls had perished. They had all seen the bodies.

Back in England, the news spread across the country like wildfire and when it reached Bude, Dylan stopped dead in his tracks. Panic-stricken, he immediately imagined that Amelie had been one of those who were lost. How could she have possibly survived all alone? Thinking the survivors list would not be published for some time, Dylan wracked his brains wondering how he could find out. Crushed by the news and not knowing what to do, he fully accepted that in all probability, his beloved Amelie was gone forever.

That dreadful news aged Dylan overnight and fearing the worst, he sank into a depression and lost all interest in his own life. Instead, he threw himself into the farm and worked so hard that he would collapse into bed every night, exhausted. But there was no respite, as his dreams invented images of Amelie in the freezing water, crying for help, with nobody there to save her. The dreams became nightmares and Dylan looked older each day, lacking in sleep, with little will to continue living. There was nothing anyone could say or do to comfort him, it was as though he too was a lost soul of the Titanic.

Amelie and Ruby-Jane, along with hundreds of their fellow survivors, slept on the open deck for three nights. The weather was cruel and the storms lashed the Carpathia, causing even more misery for its passengers and crew. The Captain was worried, they did not have enough blankets to keep everyone warm and that damned rain just would *not* let up. Pneumonia was a big worry. Everyone on board prayed for their safe passage to America's shores.

Four days later, as the Carpathia arrived in New York, tens of thousands of people stood watching and waving them in. Despite the evening rain, which was incessant, many people were there to offer help. Individuals, charities and many different women's groups all provided assistance and support to those who did not have families to travel onwards to. Grateful for the help they were being shown, many of the survivors were relieved just to finally be stood on solid ground. All they needed for the immediate time, was to get warm and eat a hot meal. Many New Yorkers opened their homes to survivors. It was as if the whole of New York had turned out to help them all. That alone, was a blessing the survivors would never forget.

There would of course be investigations into the cause of why the unsinkable RMS Titanic, actually did do the unthinkable, the Captain of the Carpathia had warned them all of that fact, via his crew, when they had gathered everyone's name for the ship's log. Amelie and Ruby-Jane both agreed there would likely be repercussions that none of them would ever know of, but for now, all that mattered was that they were safe. It was true for them, New York had never before, been such a welcome sight from ship to shore.

As Amelie and Ruby-Jane off-boarded, they were welcomed by the Red Cross, who took charge of the two young children they had been caring for. The children were from New York themselves, but both were still so shocked and over-tired, they could only repeat their first names. Amelie and Ruby-Jane passed on the information they had gleaned from little Tommy and Charlotte, who, as it turned out, were brother and sister, aged just five and six, and very well spoken, having come from a wealthy family, which could afford the Governess they had become separated from on Titanic's deck. In her own search to find them, their Governess had not survived and sadly, neither had their parents. The two youngsters were now orphans. Thankfully, the Red Cross reassured Amelie and Ruby-Jane, that because they would have been registered correctly on the official passenger list, their families would be traced and eventually reunited with little Tommy and Charlotte.

Wandering through the crowds of survivors now streaming off the ship, Amelie and Ruby-Jane found themselves passing a section of the dock where passengers were on stretchers and as Amelie glanced across the two rows, she spotted a familiar face.

"Alfie? Oh, my gosh, Alfie!" Amelie grabbed Ruby-Jane's arm as she excitedly exclaimed, "He's alive! Alfie!"

On hearing his name, their rescuer, Alfie, moved his head to one side, the cold water had dropped his body temperature so low that onboard the Carpathia, he had been taken straight to one of the cabins, which is why, when Amelie and Ruby-Jane had searched the survivors on deck, they had not found him. Relief and joy at finding Alfie alive, washed over them as they took his hands and said how happy they were to find him there. Alfie, although pleased to see his friends alive, was more worried for his wife and asked if they would kindly go to her, to let her know he was safe and that he would be home as soon as he could walk again. The Red Cross had told him he would be transferred to hospital, for they were certain he was suffering the effects of hypothermia and needed to be treated properly before he could be released to go home.

Amelie and Ruby-Jane were so happy to find Alfie alive, that they were glad to go and re-assure his wife and look in on his new-born son. Promising Alfie they would go straight there, despite the late hour, the two women also promised him they would be back the following day to check on him.

Luckily Ruby-Jane knew the area quite well where Alfie lived, for her own employer, Ms Marjorie Madison, lived in the same area and Ruby-Jane herself, lived not far from it. As Ms Madison popped into her head again, Ruby-Jane wondered if she had also been saved? After all, she *was* travelling in first class with her gentleman friend, so Ruby-Jane had automatically assumed she was safe, thinking the first-class passengers would have been given priority in the lifeboats. Now though, because they themselves were safely back in New York and beginning to recover from the effects of that dreadful night, Ruby-Jane became more worried and urgently wanted to find out what had happened to her employer, praying that Ms Madison had survived. The shock of the past four days had thrown everyone into a state of confusion and with normal life seemingly so distant, Ruby-Jane felt guilty for not having thought too much about Ms Madison, but she had been in shock herself and worried for little Tommy and Charlotte, as well as Amelie and of course, poor Alfie. Deciding to go to Ms Madison's house as soon as she was able, calmed Ruby-Jane a little, but with Ms Madison having no living family, there would be nobody to check on her except Ruby-Jane, who was really the only person that Marjorie Madison had, other than the polite society that surrounded her whenever she graced a social occasion. A wave of sadness for Ms Maddison, suddenly overwhelmed Ruby-Jane and hanging on to Amelie's arm as they made their way to a waiting taxi, she began to cry. Amelie tried to comfort her new friend, but was so exhausted herself, that she too began to weep, mainly for those poor souls who did not survive, but also for herself and her own loss, which still bubbled to the surface whenever she was over-wrought. Knowing the survivors had no money, many of New York's taxi drivers had offered onward journeys free of charge, provided they were within New York itself. A kind and generous offer, which both Amelie and Ruby-Jane were extremely grateful for themselves, but even so, they asked for the driver's name and address, promising to repay him as soon as they were able. The driver told them not to worry, that he was happy to help, but as they were so insistent, he told them the address, without believing they would remember it.

As the car pulled up outside Alfie's house, there were very few lights on, the hour was late and they expected Alfie's wife to already be in bed asleep. Which, normally, would have deterred a late calling, but on this occasion, they believed Alfie's wife would be only too happy to have her sleep disturbed. As it turned out, sleep was the last thing Mollie Davidson could do. Having heard the most dreadful news about RMS Titanic, Alfie's wife had worried herself sick about her husband and despite having their new-born son to look after, she had thought of nothing else since the news first broke. Sleep-deprived and exhausted with worry, on hearing the persistent banging on the front door and knowing her housekeeper would get to answer it before she herself could make it downstairs, Mollie slipped out of bed and pulled on a warm dressing-gown over her cotton nightdress. Anxious for news of Alfie and assuming the banging would be the police, or similar, Mollie ran downstairs barefoot, only to find that Martha had indeed already reached the door and swung it open, a worried look on her face. Seeing two young women stood on the doorstep without warm coats and looking very dishevelled, even in the semi-darkness, all Martha could say was, "Yes? Can I help you?"

Amelie spoke first, advising that they have important

news for Mrs Mollie Davidson, news of her husband Alfie. On hearing this as she reached the bottom of the stairs, Mollie called out to Martha to let them in. Shocked at the appearance of the two young women, Mollie ushered them into the still-warm parlour and asked Martha to fetch blankets and to please make some tea for them all. As the women sat by the dying fire-embers, soaking in the warmth, Amelie told the desperate Mollie, that Alfie was still alive and not only that, but that he was a true hero, who had saved many lives, including their own, and those of the two children they had watched over. At this news, the stress and worry that Mollie had held inside ever since hearing of the disastrous sinking of Titanic, erupted into relief and joy, mixed with tears, followed by almost hysterical laughter as she hugged both women, thanking them profusely for the best news ever!

Feeling happy, if not a little overwhelmed by Mollie's gratitude, the two young women, now wrapped in a blanket each, found themselves smiling again, something they had not done since sharing that last dinner onboard with Alfie. As they began to relay the story of how they had all met and gotten to know Alfie, the women finally relaxed and seeing Martha walking back in with hot tea, felt a blessed relief at being safe. Thanking her, a relieved and very proud Mollie confirmed to Martha that Master Alfie had not only survived, but was being hailed a hero. Martha and Mollie hugged each other, relief washing over them both, as their employer-employee relationship showed the strong friendship that had grown between the two of them over the past few days. They all talked into the small hours and before they knew it, Baby William was waking for his 2 a.m. feed.

Shocked by the late hour, Mollie invited both women to stay the night, offering them a room each and use of the bathroom, to bathe and change into fresh nightgowns, which she would loan to them, along with a clean dress for the following morning. Mollie was a wealthy woman and would have given her fortune away for Alfie to be safe. So, helping his friends, whom she hoped would become *their* friends, was the very least she could do and she was more than happy to look after them both for the night. Luckily for them all, the three women were about the same height and build so, sharing Mollie's clothes was an easy solution. Martha showed the women to their rooms, once they had all looked in on William and having left Mollie alone to feed him, they again thanked Martha and disappeared into their bedrooms.

Despite her immense wealth, Mollie had wanted to look after William herself and so, she had not yet engaged a Nanny. That night, as she cuddled her new-born son to her breast, never before had she felt so elated, Alfie was safe and William would get to meet his Daddy tomorrow, for she would join Amelie and Ruby-Jane when they travelled back to the hospital.

As Ruby-Jane and Amelie settled down for the night, the dawn was almost breaking, such was the late hour, but they were happy... alive, safe, and yes, extremely happy for Mollie, Alfie and little William. Sleep took over them instantly and they slept for nine hours solid, only waking when William's cries drifted along the corridor as Mollie carried him downstairs from his morning nap.

Awakening to such a joyful sound did not prevent the memories from flooding back in, but this time they were soothed by the sound of Mollie and Alfie's little son, whom they already felt bonded to. Mainly due to the excited daddy-talk oozing out of Alfie, whenever he spoke of Mollie and William on the ship. Quickly rising, the two women freshened up and slipped into the clothes that

Mollie had kindly loaned them. It was good to feel clean again and to have slept in a real bed.

Martha heard the ladies moving around upstairs and had already prepared a late breakfast for them. Knowing they too would be keen to go to Alfie's bedside immediately. Martha had also used the new house telephone to call for a taxi to take them to the hospital that Alfie was in. How lucky they were, that Alfie was being so well cared for, when there must be hundreds of people needing medical attention. Martha gave up a silent prayer of her own, thankful that her Master and his friends had been saved.

Ruby-Jane had decided it would be best for her to call into her employer's house, when they returned from the hospital and was just informing Amelie and Mollie of her plans when a motor-car pulled into the driveway. Thinking it was their taxi, all four women immediately got up to put on their borrowed coats and wraps. Martha glanced through the window to signal to the taxi-driver, only to find it wasn't their taxi after all as she exclaimed excitedly, "It's the Master!"

Mollie flew out of her chair and ran to the front door, throwing it open and rushing into Alfie's open arms, hugging him for the longest time. Alfie laughed before kissing his wife passionately, holding her to him, telling her he had thought he might never see her again, or ever get to meet little William.

Mollie, was laughing with joy and happiness, in-between explaining how they were about to be on their way to see him. Hugging him again, she was ecstatic and Alfie was relieved and grateful that Mollie had received his message. On hearing that Amelie and Ruby-Jane had actually stayed for the night and were inside, Alfie was both relieved and over-joyed, these two women had become so important to him after their shared ordeal, that Alfie felt they would remain friends forever.

As Mollie and Alfie stepped back inside the house, Amelie and Ruby-Jane politely waited to greet him, leaving husband and wife to their private moment, only to then abandon all social etiquette as Alfie walked into the room and hugs were given all round, even for Martha, who blushed and offered her grateful thanks for Alfie's safe return. Alfie explained to them all how, amazingly, he had recovered quickly overnight, just from being kept warm in hospital and receiving hot drinks and food brought in by well-wishers, wanting to help in whatever way they could. Pneumonia was still a risk, but other than feeling exhausted from his ordeal, he was remarkably well. Knowing his wife and baby were waiting for him though, Alfie explained he could wait no longer and had discharged himself from the care of the hospital doctors, on the promise he would report to his own medical doctor the moment he was home. The hospital had been overwhelmed with injured survivors, so to have a bed come free was a welcome blessing and they allowed Alfie to leave before the doctor's rounds had even finished.

Sitting Alfie down beside the freshly made-up fire, Mollie went across the room to pick up William, who was lying quietly in his portable crib, aware of voices and smiling away to himself. Beaming with pride, Mollie turned back to Alfie and placed their son into his arms. Alfie's heart melted and immediately filled with a love he had never before known. As he looked at his new-born son, Alfie thanked Mollie for bringing him such joy and happiness, stating that no man could ever feel happier than he did right now. With so much emotion overflowing, all four women, found themselves glassy-eyed as they watched this most precious of moments, little William being cradled by his hero father, Alfie Davidson.

With Alfie home and needing time with his family, Amelie and Ruby-Jane thanked Mollie for her kind loan of clothing and her generous hospitality, before bidding them both goodbye, with promises made to visit in a few days.

Ruby-Jane needed to check-up on Ms Marjorie Madison and Amelie, who had nowhere else to go anyway, offered to accompany her. The distance was not too far, but Mollie insisted they take a taxi, which she gave them money for, as well as enough money to keep them going for a week. Such was her generous and extremely kind nature. Alfie surely had found a genuine pearl when he had met his darling Mollie.

As the taxi pulled into the gardens of Ms Madison's home, Amelie gasped, it seemed that everyone she had met so far was *very* wealthy. Whilst appreciating their good fortune, she did also worry a little and wondered how she would compare, as a relatively non-wealthy person. Thinking in terms of class had never really been in Amelie's thoughts before, but these beautiful houses and very rich people, were making her doubt herself a little, whilst also hoping she would be accepted, without too many questions asked. As Ruby-Jane lifted and released the heavy door-knocker, she explained that Ms Madison had a new housekeeper who also lived-in, so it would likely be her who would answer the door shortly. Just as those words left Ruby-Jane's mouth, the door opened and Dorothea screamed with delight at seeing their Ruby-Jane safe and well, albeit, looking less like her usual self. Ruby-Jane laughed and hugged Dorothea, whom she had grown very close to over the past few months. The question of Ms Madison's return was raised immediately their embrace relaxed.

"Has Ms Madison returned home yet, Dorothea?" Ruby-Jane prayed for good news, but as Dorothea's smile faded, the answer became obvious.

"No, Ms Ruby, there has been no word, but I scanned the names of the dead that they have released already and she is not on it, so I am hopeful that she did survive. Were you not together when it happened?" Dorothea was confused and suddenly remembering her manners, invited the two women into the sitting-room, which is where Ruby-Jane was used to being, although usually, with their mistress.

Having introduced Amelie to Dorothea, Ruby-Jane then explained what had happened in London, with Ms Madison's gentleman friend and then when they boarded RMS Titanic, how Amelie had generously shared her cabin when Ms Madison was taken ill (Ruby decided to keep to the original story to retain Ms Madison's privacy over her gentleman-friend). The telling of their awful story went on for a while, in-between taking tea and before they knew it, the afternoon had flown by. Ruby-Jane reassured Dorothea and suggested they were not to worry, that word would soon be sent and they should just wait it out. It was easier to say than do, for both women were very fond of Marjorie Madison. Promising to check back the following day, Ruby-Jane bade Dorothea a good evening, as she and Amelie left to make their way back to Ruby-Jane's apartment. Grateful for the food-parcel Dorothea had quickly pulled together, they decided to make themselves a proper meal when they got back. Both feeling very thankful of the money given to them by Mollie, some of which would pay for fresh groceries tomorrow.

It suddenly hit Amelie that what was left of the money

she had been given by young Betty's parents, was now gone. Lost on Titanic. Along with all of her clothes and personal effects. The realisation was too much and Amelie suddenly began to cry, worried that she now had absolutely nothing with which to start her new life. Ruby-Jane realised how awful it must seem for Amelie and reassured her that she need not worry about finding her own place to live, because she would absolutely now be staying with Ruby-Jane for the foreseeable future.

Feeling unbelievably grateful at such a generous offer, Amelie thanked Ruby-Jane again, saying she was a life-saver herself and that Amelie would be lost without her support.

Reaching the apartment block, Ruby-Jane was glad to see their Building Manager, affectionally known as Georgie by all of the residents, because they would need his help to gain entry to her apartment. As the two young women stepped out of their taxi and walked towards the front entrance, Ruby-Jane received a beaming smile from Georgie, who was relieved to see his smiling young tenant safe and well.

"Oh, Miss Ruby, it is so good to see you again, it has been such a worrying time, waiting for news of the passengers lost on the ship."

"Georgie, oh my, how lovely of you to be so concerned, it is wonderful to see you too. I have to admit, I thought I might never make it back."

Unexpectedly, for Georgie, Ruby-Jane greeted him like an old friend. It seemed that the ordeal of losing so many fellow passengers at sea, had given her a new sense of belonging and a love for the people she knew. Georgie, of course, had heard the news and had been keeping everything crossed that his lovely, smiling Ruby-Jane would be among the survivors. He had even placed fresh flowers on the hall-table outside her apartment door, hoping she would be home to enjoy them soon. Seeing the women looking a little jaded and hearing the barest of explanations, Georgie re-assured Ruby-Jane that he would sort out fresh keys for them both and not to worry, they could explain everything tomorrow. For now, he would let them in and was just mightily relieved that they were safe and well, considering what the alternative could have been.

Thankful of finally reaching Ruby-Jane's home, *now her home too*, Amelie took in a deep breath as she entered and said, "Wow!"

Ruby-Jane had not previously shared any details of what her home was like and Amelie had imagined a small apartment, but this was huge! So much bigger and quite frankly, grander than she had ever imagined. It hadn't even dawned on Amelie to imagine what it would be like, when Ruby-Jane first mentioned that Ms Madison provided the apartment. Of course, when she had seen how wealthy Ms Madison obviously was, she had expected the apartment would be in a reasonably good area, but this was beyond even her wildest dreams.

"Oh, my goodness Ruby-Jane, this is spectacular and just look at the view!" Amelie crossed the room to look through the huge windows, which, during the daylight hours allowed sunshine to flood in. In this twilight though, Amelie could see that the apartment overlooked a huge park, which was so unexpected that she was lost for words. Ruby-Jane just laughed, having not given it a second thought, this was just her home, but of course, she had no idea of what Amelie's own home had been like, back in England. Ruby-Jane showed Amelie around, including the bedroom, which would now become hers and when Amelie begged the question of, "However can I repay you?" Ruby-Jane just said they could sort things like that out at a later date, once Amelie was back on her feet. For now, they just needed to eat, bathe and get to bed. Laughing with blessed relief, the two friends did exactly that. Their meal was simple, but delicious, because they were home and most importantly, safe.

Chapter 5

Starting Over

The following day, saw Ruby-Jane sorting out Amelie with some of her clothes, to help her get started and to ensure she had a decent outfit to wear for her first interview - both women assuming there would be one soon - New York was, after all, a more liberal society, that was open to women working to earn their own living, rather than relying on a man to provide it for them. At least, that had been Amelie's understanding, but it was an assumption she would quickly realise as being somewhat mis-guided. Amelie would however, feel eternally grateful to Ruby-Jane, because if it were not for her and Mollie, Amelie would be both homeless and penniless right now.

As well as introducing Amelie to a few friendly neighbours in their apartment building, Ruby-Jane enjoyed showing her new friend around their local area, and was bemused by the awe and excitement that Amelie's fresh eyes saw in even the most mundane of places. Amelie marvelled at everything that seemed bigger and brighter than she had expected, and was certainly the very opposite end of the spectrum compared to her home-town, back in England. Thinking briefly of Bude, as the two friends walked into Central Park, Amelie remarked to Ruby-Jane that she must write to Dylan to explain she had arrived and was now well, and already making friends. Not realising that Dylan had already heard about the Titanic and assumed she was lost on that terrible night, Amelie decided to leave writing her letter until the following week, thinking it would give her time to seek work and hopefully write with some good news. Aware of the fact that she had little to no money now, the need for finding work was all the more urgent. As the two women chatted about this dilemma, Amelie remembered Alfie mentioning his friend who worked for the New York Times.

Ruby-Jane, who had not been a party to that conversation, immediately encouraged Amelie to contact Alfie and follow-up on his offer. If it worked out well for Amelie, such an introduction could be the miracle she felt she now needed, to kick-start her new working life.

Luckily, confidence was something that Amelie was not lacking in and she felt sure that given an introduction, she could convince an Editor to give her a try. After all, this was New York and not a sleepy little English town. Amelie also quickly realised that she would likely have to prove herself to be twice as good as a man, to be thought of as anything close to being equally skilled.

Whilst times were definitely changing, thanks to the efforts of the suffragette movement and the admirable Emmaline Pankhurst – who championed the rights of women to vote – women were still not regarded as equal, meaning many men in the workplace still regarded women as lower-level workers, not deserving of equal respect, or position. Amelie would need to prove her worth, of that she was now very well aware. It was a battle she was ready to fight though, determined as she was, to succeed in her new life.

As the two friends strolled through the park, Ruby-Jane suggested they call on Alfie and Mollie the following day, to ask Alfie about his contact at the New York Times.

Amelie was feeling enthusiastic and excited, and having Ruby-Jane's support was truly appreciated. The two women had surprised themselves by the close bond they had already developed. So much so, that Ruby-Jane had suggested Amelie just call her Ruby, saying she was becoming quite tired of her double-barrelled name, feeling it seem so old-fashioned in today's modern society. Amelie had laughed and said she thought it sounded super-chic to just be called Ruby and reminded her of the very precious stone that her name represented. Ruby was cheered by Amelie's comments and decided that she would also ask Ms Marjorie Madison to just call her Ruby. Speaking about her employer, Ruby said she would call on the house to see if there was any news. The walk would do them both good and the Spring sunshine encouraged them to stay outside, enjoying the warmth of the sun on their skin.

As the two friends approached Ms Madison's house, a large vehicle which had been parked in the driveway, suddenly pulled away. The gravel of the driveway crunched under its wheels, warning them of its approach as they turned into the entrance, but even then, only missing Ruby by just a few inches. Catching her arm to prevent her from falling backwards, Amelie called out to the driver to be more careful, but he had not even realised the presence of the two women and drove away, none-the-wiser from his close encounter. Feeling a little shaken, Ruby assured Amelie she was not hurt, despite her friend's surprisingly strong grip.

"It's okay, I'm fine Amelie, thanks to you and please don't worry about bruising, it could have been so much worse, had you not held onto me."

Ruby smiled at Amelie and as they reached the front door, she pulled on the bell-chord, enjoying the musical jangling of the bell just inside. It was taking a good while for Dorothea to come to the front entrance so, Ruby suggested they walk around the back of the house to the kitchen door; which was normally only used by tradespeople and the staff who helped to keep Dorchester House looking so smart and tidy. Ruby generally used the front door herself, but was not averse to using the tradesman's entrance, particularly as she was slightly concerned about what the large vehicle had been there for.

Making their way through the kitchens and into the hallway, Ruby startled Dorothea when she called out, having seen the house-keeper walking down the sweeping staircase.

"Oh, Ms Ruby, Ms Amelie I didn't realise you had arrived."

"Hello Dorothea, yes, sorry, we used the kitchen entrance, having seen a large vehicle driving out, is Ms Madison home, is she well?" Ruby had so many questions, she almost bombarded Dorothea with them.

"Yes, Ms Ruby, Ms Madison is home and now in bed. It seems her arm was broken when a man fell on her, as he tried to move along the lifeboat in his panic. Apparently, she passed out from the pain and of course, wearing only her ballgown, quickly succumbed to the cold. Thankfully, the doctor on the Carpathia, managed to fashion a sling, but he was unable to re-set her arm. So, the hospital doctors have now done that and once they were certain she had recovered well enough from the hypothermia, they allowed her to go home. Mind you, the mistress told me she was insistent on being allowed home, not wanting to spend a moment longer than was necessary in the hospital and having the good fortune to have her own doctor on call, she felt she would recover better in her own bed." Dorothea was pleased at her recount of the chain of events, before then offering Ruby and Amelie

53

some tea.

Both women thanked Dorothea, gratefully accepting her kind offer. Ruby added that she would just run upstairs to see Ms Madison and ask if there was anything that she could do for her. Ruby suggested Amelie wait in the front parlour, whilst Dorothea made the tea. Amelie didn't mind at all, saying she would take a look at the inviting book collection beside the fireplace.

The parlour was a beautiful room and Amelie loved the simple, yet comforting warmth it offered. Spotting a copy of 'The Phantom of the Opera', a very excited Amelie gently took it from the shelf, marvelling at the fact that she was holding a copy of this beautiful new book in her own hands. Amelie had never held a brand-new book such as this before, let alone one that had only recently been released, so this was a real treat and she was very careful not to damage it in any way, as she gently turned the first pages.

When Dorothea arrived with a tea-tray laden with cakes as well as cups and saucers, Amelie reluctantly returned the book back to its shelf, promising herself that one day, she too would own a copy of this intriguing work of fiction. Dorothea poured some tea into a cup for Amelie and handed it to her, offering milk and sugar. Pouring another cup for Ruby-Jane, she added one lump of sugar, having learned of the younger woman's sweet tooth soon after joining the household. Excusing herself to take the mistress a tray, Dorothea suggested Amelie help herself to whichever cake most appealed and then disappeared off to the kitchen. Ruby returned from upstairs a few moments later.

"Well, that was an emotional reunion, I feel quite wrung out." Ruby went on to explain that Ms Madison was relieved and very happy to see Ruby-Jane alive, as was she for her employer, albeit with a broken arm. They had both agreed a broken arm seemed a small price to pay, considering how much worse the outcome could have been. Ms Madison was devastated at the loss of her gentleman friend though and whilst pleased to see Ruby-Jane, she now wanted to be left alone for the afternoon, to privately grieve his loss. Seeing her so exhausted and needing a good rest, Ruby assured Ms Madison, that the rest of the day in bed was probably for the best and that she would return in the morning, to assist her to bathe and dress. Ruby wasn't going to allow her to wallow for too long, knowing how bad that situation would be for her wellbeing and with one arm out of action, Marjorie Madison accepted she was going to have to be quite dependant on her young companion over the coming weeks. Appreciating Ruby-Jane's ongoing support and kindness, Ms Madison thanked her for stopping by and suggested Ruby-Jane bring Amelie back another time, to meet her properly. Following a final request before she left the room, Marjorie Madison also agreed to now call her companion, Ruby, at which the younger woman beamed with delight. Insisting Ruby and Amelie enjoy some tea before they left, Marjorie added that she would look forward to seeing Ruby in the morning, although, not too early. The two women agreed that a lie-in was definitely needed.

Marjorie Madison laid back against her pillows and closed her eyes. Frowning, as the instant visions of her darling Benjamin – who remained onboard to ensure there was a place in the lifeboat for her – flooded into her mind again. In the privacy of her bedroom, the tears could now flow unchecked and so they did, for the rest of that day, until sleep finally overtook her exhausted mind in the very early hours of the following day.

That morning, Ruby and Amelie arose at the same time, and shared a light breakfast, neither having ever really developed a habit for breakfasting on a large meal. Ruby asked Amelie what she would do whilst Ruby went off to attend to Ms Madison. Thinking about work, Amelie said she would take a walk to explore a little, whilst also heading in the direction of Alfie and Mollie's house. Ruby agreed it was a good plan and said she would meet her there, as soon as she was finished with Ms Madison. Not expecting to be wanted to stay-on all day, in view of her employer's need for privacy to grieve. However, Ruby confirmed that should Ms Madison want her to stay, Amelie was to go ahead and continue her discussions with Alfie, oh, and to also let Mollie and Alfie know that Ruby would visit them very soon.

Having sent Ruby off with good wishes for a pleasant time with Ms Madison, Amelie left the apartment, having let Georgie know where she was headed to, in case she got lost and they had to come looking for her, to which, he just laughed and wished her a lovely day. Georgie felt sure, that this confident and delightful young woman, was perfectly capable of finding her way around New York, despite being from out of town. In fact, he suspected that her beauty and interesting British accent, would intrigue and invite assistance from all quarters. Amelie smiled at his kind suggestion, thinking what a nice man he was. Of course, Amelie did not really see herself as beautiful, indeed, she felt quite ordinary inside her head, but she did always try to make an effort to look pleasing on the eye and felt it was her smile that attracted most attention. Caden had always loved her smile, but then, he had loved every inch of her, from the tip of her nose to her pretty little toes.

Setting off on her little adventure, Amelie enjoyed the

walk to Alfie and Mollie's house and prayed they would be happy for her to call so unexpectedly. Remembering their previous kind offer to call any time, Amelie hoped that she would find them both at home.

As it turned out, Marjorie Madison did want Ruby to stay with her that day, she had exhausted herself crying over Benjamin, but now needed to talk to someone about him. Having realised the very likeable Ruby had become someone she regarded as a friend, as well as her employed companion, Marjorie wanted to share her secret with Ruby, particularly, knowing that Ruby had also met Benjamin Grigson and seen what a charming man he had been, and how he had taken quite a shine to Ms Madison.

Their decision to book adjoining cabins, whilst a little unorthodox in such circumstances, had been a blessing and Ms Madison had enjoyed intimate relations with him during their brief, but precious time onboard RMS Titanic. The beauty of the ship, the excitement of their developing love and his extremely attractive, and charismatic persona, had completely won over Marjorie Madison, ever since she had first laid eyes upon Benjamin Grigson. So, when he spoke to her of marriage, she had been very willing to accept his proposal. Being a man of tradition, Benjamin felt that in order to make his proposal official, he needed to take her to Tiffany's to purchase a diamond engagement ring of her choice, before they made any such announcement to New York's Society. But it had been during their third night of steamy passion, that he could wait no longer and as he caressed her naked body, gently kissing and stroking her most private of places, Benjamin's lips had brushed hers and looking into her beautiful blue eyes, he had shared his thoughts... here she was, this remarkable, yet beautiful woman, who was strong and independent, experienced in life and yet, seemingly so innocent, who could make him laugh and feel proud, and he desperately wanted her to become his wife. No, he *needed* her to become his wife, because he wanted to make love to her every day of their lives together and he wanted to show the world how lucky he was, to have such a witty, intelligent and extremely beautiful wife.

Marjorie, whom he had loved to call Ria, had gasped at his generous description of her, and at his touch, as he preened confidently, knowing his words were able to affect every emotion in her body. Taking her hand in his, in the romance of their luxurious bedroom, her darling Benjamin had asked that most important of questions.

"My most precious darling, Ria, I love you with all my heart and I think I will for the rest of my life, so when we reach New York, I want to announce that you, Ms Marjorie Madison, my darling Ria, have accepted my proposal of marriage. But, before I can, I need to ask you, my darling, if you will do me the very great honour of becoming my wife?"

With baited breath, Benjamin had waited, desperate for her answer and willing it to be yes. Whilst it was not the usual type of proposal that their society would expect, his darling Ria had truly captured both his heart and soul, and throughout this intense moment of waiting, he knew he wanted her to be with him, always.

Marjorie Madison had looked back at his deep brown eyes and smiled a smile so beautiful, that it melted his heart and raised his passion.

"Oh, yes. My darling Ben. I will. I most definitely will. You have made me so happy that I want to..." and before Marjorie could finish her answer, Benjamin had crushed her lips with a passionate kiss and moved his body to lie on top of her. Seeking the warmth of her most private place, his unbridled passion working them both into a steamy climax, as pressing her hands on the bed, he had watched her naked breasts moving to the rhythm of their lovemaking, smiling at her beautiful face, absorbing the enjoyment she was also feeling and then both of them groaning, as his seed shot out and planted itself deep in her belly. Benjamin had told Marjorie that he loved her to the moon and back, and that she had just made him the happiest man in the world. Overwhelmed with love for her man, Marjorie had cried tears of joy and happiness, in the knowledge that she was to become Benjamin's wife, and very soon, although she did not know it in that moment, the mother of his only child.

Of course, those detailed memories could not be shared with Ruby, but Marjorie Madison needed to tell someone who could understand and not criticise that she would have become Mrs Benjamin Grigson, had her darling Ben survived. It broke her heart that just as she had found such immense happiness, it had been cruelly snatched away. As she spoke those words, Marjorie's tears brimmed again and Ruby reached out to hold her employer in her arms, gently stroking her hair until she felt Marjorie's sobs subside.

Ruby thought how unexpected this most precious and very private moment was, and felt deeply touched when Marjorie told her that she had come to regard Ruby as a friend and confidante, rather than just her employee. Feeling a little speechless, Ruby just smiled broadly and nodded, tears springing into her own eyes at this unexpected, but welcome development in their relationship. Ruby felt desperate for Marjorie's loss of Benjamin; to have loved so briefly, yet completely, was unbearable for Marjorie and Ruby wanted to help in any way she could. Not that anything could ever take away the pain of losing the man you loved.

Through the sinking of the Titanic and the loss of so many souls, Marjorie no longer felt any importance in the class system that dogged the society she mixed in, and in fact, she wanted to be more like Ruby and become a 'modern miss'; one who was still respected by her peers, but someone that people could also reach out to and relate to. There was a long and difficult path ahead in changing the deep-rooted culture of the circles they mixed in, but, Marjorie and Ruby, felt they both should work together to start the revolution of change, equality and a less haughty society was what they dreamed of. Emmaline Pankhurst would have been proud to call them suffragettes, had she known of them.

Amelie reached Alfie and Mollie's house mid-afternoon, feeling conscious of not arriving around their lunch-time, but happy to accept late afternoon tea, as was accepted and proper in their society. That said, neither Alfie, or Mollie were precious about things like that, in spite of their wealth, they were far too modern in their thinking. Happy to see positive changes evolving, they too wanted and hoped for a more equal society.

As she was greeted at the door by their kindly housekeeper, Martha, Amelie felt immediately welcome and gratefully accepted Martha's offer to take her coat. Which was actually was one of Ruby's coats, of course, but all the same, it was kind of Martha to take it for her. Amelie heard Mollie's voice calling from the parlour to come in. Young William was having his afternoon feed and the thoroughly modern Mollie was happy for Amelie to sit with her, as she covered her naked breast with a muslin. Most of society would be shocked to know a baby was being fed in the parlour, expecting it to be taken to the nursery, but this was 1912 and Mollie knew there was only herself and Martha in the house. Having heard so much from Alfie about the English Rose, who was actually a strong and independent woman, Mollie gauged that Amelie would be comfortable with her feeding William in front of her.

Amelie walked over to Mollie to kiss her cheek and touch the back of little William's head, which was just visible from under the muslin. Seeing his feet move, Amelie took that to mean he was saying hello, but far too busy enjoying his mother's milk to trouble himself with anything more. As Amelie took the offered seat opposite Mollie, the two women began discussing everything that had happened in the past few days. Obvious good-health questions aside, Mollie was interested to know how Amelie was settling-in to life in New York and of course, to Ruby-Jane's apartment. Amelie happily shared her experience of the past couple of days and confirmed that Ms Marjorie Madison had returned home, safely, albeit with a broken arm. Mollie was over-joyed for Ruby-Jane and said what wonderful news it was. Obviously, not knowing Ruby-Jane's employer, Mollie could offer no more than that, but knowing how concerned Ruby-Jane had been, she was very happy and relieved to learn of another survivor. Amelie also told Mollie of Ruby's decision to have her friend's call her by just her first name of Ruby. Both of them agreed it sounded quite chic, compared to the fuller, Ruby-Jane. Mollie agreed and said she would let Alfie know too, so they could all use Ruby's new, shortened name.

The two women traded updates and shared tea, whilst they awaited Alfie's return from work. As it turned out, Alfie wasn't just a Chief Engineer, he and Mollie actually owned the company. Amelie thought how unassuming and wonderfully normal this obviously extremely wealthy couple were. It was quite refreshing to Amelie, having seen several examples of poor social etiquette and behaviours amongst the upper classes whilst onboard Titanic.

As Mollie finished William's feeding regime and re-dressed her naked breasts, she offered William to Amelie for a cuddle, which was readily accepted. Amelie, having already fallen in love with their little bundle of joy, remarked on what a blessing he was and how lucky they were to be his parents. Amelie's own previously suppressed biological needs began to bubble to the surface and as she held little William, her body reacted in a way she had not previously experienced. Amelie had wanted a baby with Caden, but sadly they had never been successful in their attempts, which had frustrated them both, yet, in an unexpected way, their inability to have a baby together had also cemented their love for one another, making it all the more special.

As William drifted off into his post-feed sleep, Amelie wished for a moment that she too, had a small bundle of joy. Then quickly dismissed it, knowing her plans to work at the newspaper could not possibly include a baby. Having her thoughts so abruptly switched over to work-mode, Amelie mentioned about Alfie's kind offer, to introduce her to his reporter friend at the New York Times.

"Oh, yes, Alfie told me all about that and I believe he was calling his friend today. Apparently, the newspaper is expanding so rapidly, they're looking for several people and Alfie seemed to think you might be lucky, provided they don't say no because you're a woman."

Mollie went on to speak about the injustices of women not being able to vote, or be regarded as equal in the workplace. It was something she also felt very strongly about, despite not needing to work herself. Amelie completely agreed.

"Now, Amelie, as you know, Alfie and I have more money than we need, so I hope you won't be offended if I offer you a helping hand? I know Ruby has been an absolute gem in sharing her apartment with you, but I also know you lost everything, including all your clothes. I've been thinking of having a clear-out of my wardrobe, partly due to having not been able to wear so many of my clothes since before this little one arrived, but also because I feel I need to treat myself to something new and it will make me feel better about myself, and my new shape. So, if someone such as yourself could make good use of my beautiful clothes and look stunning for me, that would make me even happier."

Mollie laughed in such a casual and friendly way that Amelie was overwhelmed by her kindness, whilst rebuking Mollie for her self-deprecating comment. In truth, Mollie would look good in whatever she wore, as far as Amelie was concerned and she told her so, as she also thanked Mollie for her amazing and very kind generosity. Hugging her kind friend and benefactor, Amelie also thanked Mollie for caring so much about her and Ruby.

Whilst Mollie felt hugely rewarded in being able to help someone less fortunate than herself, because it was Amelie, whom she and Alfie both regarded as a friend, it was all the more special. Arranging for Amelie to come back the following week to help Mollie sort through her wardrobe, she also invited Amelie and Ruby to join her and Alfie for dinner too. Amelie graciously thanked Mollie again, feeling overwhelmed by the kindness she had received since landing in New York.

Just then, Alfie returned from work and calling out to Mollie, he was delighted to find Amelie with her. Indeed, it was perfect timing he said, for he had spoken to his reporter friend. Stan Lander actually held a very senior position at the paper and having heard that Amelie was English, and had run her own small newsletter-come-newspaper in England, had told Alfie, he would undoubtedly be able to influence the Editor to take a chance on Amelie. The only condition was that Stan wanted to meet her first, for an informal interview and would also ask her to provide a written article on a specific topic, that he would tell her about on the day. Amelie was to meet with him the day after tomorrow, at ten o'clock in the morning. Alfie beamed with delight and said Amelie should be ready to work her magic and impress the hell out of him. Stan Lander, was second-in-command to the Editor and Amelie was to meet him in the foyer of their building on Longacre Square.

Amelie really could not believe her luck, Alfie and Mollie, as well as Ruby, had all opened their hearts and homes to her, helping her to get started on this new life adventure and she would never forget their kind generosity. Verbalising this to Alfie and Mollie, made them respect Amelie even more, whilst also dismissing their own efforts as 'no big deal'. Having quickly gotten used to the behaviours of some members of New York's upper-class society, Alfie had forgotten just how genuinely thankful and polite, so many English people could be, when even a small kindness was offered. As for himself, Alfie was truly happy to be able to help a fellow countryman, or woman, in this case. Amelie promised to report back to them both, once she had met with Stan Lander and asked that they keep their fingers crossed for her.

Chapter 6

New York Times

Amelie felt nervous excitement on the morning of her meeting with Stan Lander and got up far earlier than she needed to, her sleep having been disturbed by the worries and concerns she was feeling, as well as the excited anticipation. Wanting to impress, but keen to be offered a position based on merit and not just because she was Alfie's friend, Amelie wondered what the topic would be that she would need to write about. Feeling too nervous to eat, Amelie relented when Ruby pointed out that having her tummy rumble whilst she was with Stan Lander, might not make the best of impressions and quickly cut a slice of bread and some cheese, washing it all down with a glass of milk. Chatting to Ruby about her thoughts around what kind of article she would like to write, Amelie found herself thinking about her life back in Bude, wondering if a story about English life might suffice. Realising the time and not wanting to arrive hot and bothered, Amelie accepted Ruby's good-luck hug and compliments on how smart she looked in her borrowed dress before she rushed out of the door, her coat thrown around her shoulders, then slipping her arms into the sleeves, being careful not to bang her elbow on the elevator door as she stepped into it. Georgie was on duty when Amelie reached the foyer and wishing him a pleasant morning, she also asked him to wish her luck as she flew out of the front doors. Georgie, not knowing what he was wishing her luck for, just shouted out, "Good luck Ms Amelie!" Waving her arm in acknowledgement, Amelie set-off towards Longacre Square. The streets were already becoming busy, with people going to and fro, in their rush to get to work and Amelie suddenly felt quite at home. Thinking she was fast becoming a true resident of New York, albeit one with a very English accent, as she made her way along the streets, taking care at the intersections, Amelie's spirits were high. New York traffic was certainly busier than Bude, that was for sure, she had never seen so many cars on one street. Even the horse-drawn carriages were out-numbered.

As Amelie pushed through the revolving door of the New York Times office, she was pleasantly surprised at how welcoming it felt to her, almost as if she had been there before. Of course, she hadn't, but the feeling was so strong that almost too quickly, she dismissed the possibility of having lived a previous life in New York as fanciful. Amelie walked across to the receptionist and gave her name, explaining that she was there to meet Stan Lander.

"Ah, yes, Amelie Trewin. Mr Lander is expecting you. Please take a seat and I will let him know you have arrived."

The receptionist was efficient and friendly, which caused Amelie to relax a little, already feeling her earlier concerns beginning to melt away. It just felt so right for her to be there, that Amelie began to imagine she had already been offered the role.

Ten minutes later, a tall and wiry Stan Lander rushed out of the elevator, pen and papers in hand, looking a little dishevelled and raising his eyebrows as if pleasantly surprised. Stan approached Amelie with a smile and an approving nod of his head.

"So sorry to keep you waiting Amelie, we're working

on a massive story and I've been re-allocating reporters."

With that, Stan offered his hand to Amelie and smiled again as she returned his firm handshake. *Yes, he thought, a good start, confident handshake, well-dressed, nice face, lovely smile and well spoken. Definitely a good start.* As Stan showed Amelie through to a downstairs office, he began to ask about her reasons for coming to America. Thrown by the unexpected question, Amelie quickly recovered and explained how she had lost her husband two years previously, but had then started her local newsletter-come-newspaper in her home town of Bude (which of course, Stan had no knowledge of, having only ever heard of London and England). Amelie enthused about realising she had a greater calling and the burning desire to travel to a place more exciting than her home-town. At least that's how it had seemed to her in the beginning, but now, she realised Bude was just different, yes, a lot smaller than New York, but it was still the place she thought of as home. Seeing Stan raise his eyebrows again, Amelie quickly explained that whilst Bude would always feel like her true home, New York was her new future and it was her intention to build that future there, hence her interest in working for the paper. This made Stan feel immediately more comfortable and he asked her about the Bude newsletter and what kind of news, and articles she had covered. Amelie now relaxed completely, knowing her subject well and speaking in a very articulate manner, she gave several examples of stories she had covered. Stan was impressed, he already liked this young woman and was intrigued, both with her English accent and practical approach. *Yes, she would do nicely, if she passed the next stage.* Stan mentioned to Amelie that he would like her to write him an article of around two thousand words, about her experience on the Titanic.

"Titanic?"

"Yes, I believe you were onboard when it sank."

"Oh, how did you hear about that?"

"Alfie." Came the simple reply.

"Oh, of course, Alfie obviously told you about what happened." Amelie could have kicked herself for not realising that before voicing her question, "Well of course, I would be happy to write about my…"

Interrupting her, Stan explained a little more, "You see Amelie, as you will be aware, the story about RMS Titanic is massive, bigger than anything we've reported on for a while. Everyone wants to know about what happened. So, to have your version of events, as a survivor, would help to sell even more papers and we can use it in tomorrow's edition.

"Tomorrow?" Amelie gulped, appreciating the importance of reporting news as it happened, but not expecting to start working that day.

"Absolutely, if your piece pleases the Editor, it'll go to press tonight, so let's set you up at a desk and you can type it up. You do type, don't you?" Stan was buzzing now, his mind leaping ahead, realising he had a real-life story landing right in his lap.

"Err, yes, of course, I can type around thirty words per minute."

Amelie's own enthusiasm began to bubble inside her and feeling that nervous excitement being kicked into touch, she followed Stan into the elevator. The floor he worked on was only two up from the ground, but he rarely took the stairs. As the two of them chatted in the elevator, Stan asked Amelie to start the piece from when the alarm first sounded, which for her, was Alfie's voice calling out to herself and Ruby, whilst he was running along the corridor to their cabin, banging on every door that he passed.

Settling Amelie at a desk, Stan briefly introduced her to a couple of male reporters sat close by, explaining she was on trial and about to type up a piece on the Titanic, so he would get back to proper introductions later. Unusually, one of the men offered to fetch Amelie a coffee, which she gratefully accepted. Having only really begun to drink coffee once she had moved in with Ruby, the taste was growing on her. Mostly, she and Ruby took tea rather than coffee, but this was the working world and Amelie appreciated the difference.

Sat at the typewriter, Amelie was pleased to find it much newer than the one she had used back in Bude. The keys were not so far apart and so her fingers didn't get trapped quite so easily. As Amelie added the first sheet of paper, her mind drifted back to that fateful night. The shock and vivid memories flooded her mind, her concentration was impressive to anyone watching her. Which several of the men were doing, having never met an English Rose before, for that was how they saw her, an intriguing and beautiful, English Rose. The men assumed she must be talented, for Stan to have got her working so quickly, but time would tell and the article she wrote would be the deciding factor. They were intrigued at having a woman writing an article. It was a first for them all and besides which, she was a pretty sight in their otherwise fairly dull office.

It was lunchtime before Amelie finished and feeling happy with what she had written, also having drunk two cups of coffee, she was buzzing, partly due to the caffeine, but partly because she was doing what she loved, reporting a story. Stan took the pages and sat down with his own coffee to read it, leaving Amelie to talk to his Secretary, Julianne, who had been absent earlier, having needed to run an errand for Stan.

Julianne now did her best to make Amelie feel welcome, saying that she herself was very pleased to see another woman joining the team. Not that Stan had confirmed Amelie's engagement, but Julianne knew him well enough and had kept a close eye on his face as he was reading Amelie's article, she could tell he was already impressed. As he finished, Stan jumped up and rushed off to the Editor's office, excited at such a well-written and articulate piece. Amelie had impressed Stan and he was going to return with a job offer, should Bob concur. Bob was the Editor, a rather portly man who smoked cigars and had silver bands holding up his shirt sleeves, but a better experienced or hard-nosed Editor, Stan was yet to meet. Bob did concur, much to Stan's relief and agreed with the job offer Stan suggested. It was around thirty minutes later when Stan returned to speak to Amelie.

"Amelie, that was a fascinating account, Bob is impressed, as am I and we will definitely be including it in tonight's press."

Amelie beamed as Stan confirmed this most exciting news.

"So, we'd like you to stay for today, find your feet and settle-in, then tomorrow, you'll be writing-up some fresh articles, which we'll talk through in the morning. Your starting wage will be less than the men's, but prove yourself and we'll review it in three months." Stan was quite pragmatic as he spoke, "You'll be our first female article writer Amelie and we're taking a chance on you, so I hope you live up to our expectations."

Stan was quite surprised that Bob had been so easy to persuade, but the experienced Editor knew good writing when he saw it and he wanted to be seen to be a man of progress, so he had agreed to Amelie's engagement, but on a lower wage than the men.

Amelie knew she would be paid less and whilst that did bother her somewhat, she was grateful for the opportunity and grabbed it with both hands, voicing her thanks to Stan.

"Thank you very much Mr Lander, I won't let you down." Amelie offered Stan Lander her hand, which he was a little surprised by, but he took it and they shook on the deal.

"Call me Stan, Ms Trewin and I'll call you Amelie, that way, we'll get along just fine."

Amelie grinned at Stan, she knew this was a good opportunity for her and she couldn't wait to tell Ruby and Alfie. In fact, she would buy Alfie a special gift, as a thank you to him, for getting her the introduction. Stan walked away, shaking his head in disbelief, but pleased with himself for becoming the first man to want to hire a woman article-writer. He just hoped she lived up to his expectations and didn't let him down.

On that front, Stan would have no need to worry, for Amelie would soon become the first person to arrive in the office on the morning shift and one of the last to leave when on the late shift. Such was her determined dedication to be regarded highly enough to be promoted to lead reporter. It was a goal she dreamed of and she was very certain about achieving it. The sky was the limit for Amelie and she knew that had she tried to go for a similar job in London, she would most likely have been shown the door. New York was definitely the city of opportunity and for Amelie, it truly *would* become the golden apple.

When Amelie had arrived home, Ruby had not yet returned from Ms Madison's house. Disappointed at finding their apartment empty, when she was feeling in the mood to celebrate, Amelie decided to freshen up a little before making a meal for herself and Ruby. Feeling certain that her friend would arrive home soon, so they could celebrate her new job, Amelie decided to make something special for their meal.

Feeling excited and bursting with happiness at being offered her position at the paper, Amelie was desperate to share her news and being in such good humour, began humming a song as she chopped and prepared vegetables, and some fried chicken. It was going to be a real treat, they deserved it and her good news meant that very soon, she would be able to contribute towards the cost of her living in Ruby's apartment.

It was over an hour before Ruby's key turned in the lock and as she pushed open the door, the delicious cooking smells coming from the kitchen reached her nose.

"Hi Amelie, I'm home. Something smells good. How did you get on?" As Ruby voiced her question, she walked into the kitchen and seeing Amelie beaming at her, guessed it had been a good result.

Too excited to hold-in her news any longer and bursting with pride, Amelie explained everything that had happened, including how she had been offered a full-time job!

Ruby's reaction was of pure joy for her friend, "Oh, Amelie, that's truly wonderful news. I knew you would persuade them. You are just so confident and can tell a great story." Ruby was certain that Amelie would be a great success and told her so as the two friends hugged each other, almost dancing their happiness out at Amelie's most exciting news.

"We must tell Alfie." Ruby was so excited for Amelie, she wanted to tell the world, but Alfie needed to be the first.

"Yes, I know, I want to tell him today, but I have to work tomorrow and so I may not get the chance to see him until the weekend." Amelie had been told by Stan that he would keep her on weekday working for the time being, but that it could all change, depending on how the news came in.

"I also want to buy Alfie a thank-you gift, for introducing me to Stan. What do you think I should get for him?"

Ruby pondered for a moment, "Well, rather than a present, why don't we invite him and Mollie to have dinner with us here on Saturday. That way, we can both entertain them *and* have lots of cuddles with William too."

Ruby was full of great suggestions and Amelie thought it a fabulous idea, again feeling a sense of immense gratitude at her friend's generosity. After all, this was still Ruby's apartment and Amelie was really only lodging with her. But Ruby didn't think of Amelie in those terms and she was happy to join in the celebrations.

Plans made, the two friends decided to send a written invite in the post and once dinner had been enjoyed, they set about composing their special invitation. Ruby would post it in the morning and no doubt they would have a reply the very next day. So, timing would be perfect. Amelie was happy and knew that everything was going to work out well. Now that she also had some news to share with Dylan, she would write to him after work tomorrow.

Sure enough, the return note from Mollie stated that they would be delighted to accept such a wonderful dinner invitation and looked forward very much to meeting their new friends again.

Whilst Amelie was working and in-between her own time spent looking after Ms Madison, Ruby spent the rest of the week tidying their apartment; grocery shopping and food preparation would be Amelie's responsibilities, with her being by far, the better cook. Both were thankful that Alfie and Mollie were, despite their wealth and social status, quite normal people, who would not expect too much, knowing they were going to the girls' own home. Which, whilst glamorous in itself and situated in a stunning location, did not have the luxury of housekeeping staff.

Ms Madison had allowed Ruby to live in the apartment rent-free, as part of her wages, but said she would need to keep it clean and tidy herself. Ruby had of course accepted the offer with enthusiasm and promised to look after it to her very best ability. Having lived through the experience of Titanic's sinking, Ms Madison had also approved of Ruby's offer to have Amelie join her and had even given Ruby some extra cash to help with the additional expenses; mainly to cover the increased grocery bills that would be required whilst Amelie waited for her first wage packet.

Such was the kind generosity of Ms Madison, that Ruby was only too happy to provide the additional caring support that her employer needed, due to her injured arm. In some ways, their awful experience had actually helped both Ruby and Amelie to find new friends and experience kindness from people who would have been the last ones they would have expected help from.

Marjorie Madison had herself learnt a tough lesson and even though she had always been a kindly soul, seeing how so many people had lost everything they owned, had opened her eyes to the reality of starting again and the expense of it.

With no family based in New York, Ruby had always been grateful for the introduction to Ms Madison and her life had been a joy ever since, but this latest gesture, endeared her to Marjorie Madison all the more and she felt very protective of her employer.

Ruby's family were based in Detroit and heavily involved with the Ford Motor Company. A fact that would intrigue Alfie, what with him being an engineering person himself. Ruby made a mental note to remember to mention that to Alfie when he and Mollie came for dinner.

Without her family being in New York, but knowing they will have seen the news about the Titanic, Ruby had sent word to them immediately, to reassure them that she was safe and had met a new friend, Amelie, who was from England and who would be staying with her in New York. Ruby had also said that she would love to bring Amelie home on one of her future visits.

Chapter 7

Friends and Family

The meal with Alfie and Mollie went so much better than expected, and the four of them had a lovely evening, laughing, sharing stories and congratulating Amelie on her new position with the New York Times. Alfie was over the moon and brushed off the need for thanks, whilst saying that this dinner together had been a marvellous suggestion and more than enough thanks for helping out a friend. Mollie agreed and thanked them both for such a delightful meal, and evening.

Amelie and Ruby were so grateful of the friendship they were developing with Mollie and Alfie, and of course, little William, whom they both already adored and were keen to offer their child-minding services for. Alfie and Mollie appreciated their intention and kindness, but explained that they would be engaging a Nanny in a month's time, which would give Mollie a few more precious weeks of looking after Alfie by herself. Of course, with a live-in Nanny they would have a built-in babysitter, but Amelie and Ruby were invited to visit whenever they liked and cuddles with William would always be on offer. Besides which, they would be great company for Mollie whilst she was needing to remain close to William, to nurse him and until he was able to take solid food and could be apart from her for longer periods of time. Amelie and Ruby were overjoyed at this open invitation and decided they would definitely take up the kind offer, having been reminded they would be visiting the following weekend, for Mollie to show Amelie the clothes she had promised to her. Amelie already had in her mind to share her new clothes with Ruby, as she had so generously shared hers with Amelie, so it was agreed that they should both go along together to Mollie's wardrobe-clearing day.

It was just a few days later when Ruby finally received word from her very relieved parents, who were understandably, completely overjoyed on hearing she was among the survivors. Whilst grateful for the girls' safe return, compassion and concern was also offered for the ordeal the two of them had suffered, and the terrible sights they must have seen. Ruby's Mama wrote, suggesting that perhaps the two of them could visit for the July fourth celebrations and that, as the fourth was a Thursday, maybe they could ask to take a few days off and spend a long weekend with them. Ruby was uplifted on receiving word from her parents and loved the suggestion made by her Mama. As she relayed the invitation to Amelie, Ruby's excitement welled-up inside and a sudden longing to go home overwhelmed her. Thinking of her family, Ruby began sharing stories of home with Amelie, including the fact that her three brothers all worked for the Ford Motor Company, as did her Papa. Although, her Papa's role was far more senior and fast becoming more office-based; whereas the boys all worked in the factory and the machines they operated made various different parts of the automobile engines. Eager to share her knowledge, Ruby was proud to explain to Amelie that the completed automobile, had become known as the 'assembled car', although her family often thought of them as just, 'motor-cars'.

Excited about this upcoming mode of transport, Ruby explained how each brother aimed to own their own motor-car, one day. In the meantime, they only got to ride in the motor-cars that their father occasionally test-drove, whilst he held the position of Chief Motor Engineer. None of them had yet been allowed to drive one.

Although he was an engineer by trade, Ruby's father had grown up with Henry Ford and moved into the motor industry with him. The two were great friends who still liked to get their hands dirty, although it had to be said that more recently, the larger majority of their time was spent designing new models, which they hoped would take the new and expanding international motor industry, by storm.

Ruby fondly recounted to Amelie that even though the cost of owning such a motor-car was out of her brothers' reach at the moment, each of them were saving hard and had been informed that they would be allowed a reduction on the list price of the cars, should they ever save enough money to buy one. This was a generous benefit that Henry Ford would offer selected staff, although realistically, he also understood that very few would be able to afford such a luxurious item.

The idea of owning one's own car appealed very much to Amelie too and she said as much to Ruby. Amelie, feeling more like a fully grown tom-boy than a genteel lady and having watched Dylan's pride at driving the new tractor, was keen to jump in a motor-car herself and learn to drive it. Ruby, on the other hand, felt far less enthusiastic and said she would much prefer to be driven. Besides which, having so many men in her life back home, she accepted she would never stand a chance of being able to drive, ahead of any of them. The two friends laughed as they imagined Ruby trying to climb into the driving seat and pushing her brothers away as they tried to un-seat her.

Secretly, Ruby was thankful she would have so many drivers willing to escort her to wherever she wanted to go; that was of course, assuming she did eventually go back home to live, which at this moment in time, felt like it would be a long time into the future.

Working at the newspaper became a joy for Amelie and whilst she felt she worked harder and longer than the male reporters, and article writers, she didn't mind a bit, having realised that she was fast becoming top-dog in the reputation stakes. Amelie had already earned the greatest of respect from her co-workers, who frequently sought her opinion on a variety of subjects, hoping to pick up on her knowledge and skills, thereby improving on their own writing.

As the second month of her employment passed by, Amelie decided to broach the subject of being allowed some time-off around the July fourth public holiday, explaining to Stan about Ruby's family invitation and how keen she was to explore another place in America. Amelie pitched an idea to Stan, suggesting she would ask Ruby's Papa to introduce her, so that Amelie could seek an interview with Henry Ford, expecting the likelihood to be favourable, considering the close connection the two men shared. Writing a story about Henry Ford, the man behind the now famous motor car company and promoting their latest development in overseas trade, would help the Ford business no end, which Amelie felt certain, such a businessman would clearly see as an opportunity, and of course, it would make a great story for the paper too.

Knowing Amelie's uncanny knack of weeding out information from just about anyone, Stan agreed to her suggestion and said if she came back with a story, he would actually pay her for the Thursday and Friday.

Amelie jumped at the chance and before she knew it, plans for hers and Ruby's trip to the Carter family's July fourth celebrations, were organised and cemented. Ruby was beyond excited at the thought of seeing her family again and introducing them to Amelie, and felt sure her Papa would be happy to introduce Amelie to Uncle Henry.

Amelie herself was also excited, both at the thought of meeting Ruby's folks, but also at the opportunity to meet the great man, Henry Ford, his wife Clara and their son, Edsel, who was also involved in the family business. Feeling certain she could write a fascinating insight into the Ford family, Amelie just hoped that her request for an interview, would come to fruition, so that she could again impress both Stan and Bob, their Editor-in-Chief.

Life seemed to be fast-moving and ever-changing for Amelie, but she loved every minute of it and put her excitement down to city life. Compared to life in the Cornish seaside town of Bude, there was so much to do here, people to meet, interviews to be had and opportunities galore. In spite of the perilous journey to get here, Amelie felt as if she really had fallen on her feet.

Ruby was also going from strength to strength as Ms Marjorie Madison's companion and personal assistant, which was akin to a social secretary and personal aide. Ruby loved the social lifestyle she enjoyed with Ms Madison, which also suited her enquiring mind and she glowed with pride at her new job title. The two young women were fast becoming as eligible as the bachelors they were often introduced to. Sadly, as yet, not one of whom stood out from the crowd well enough to attract their undying attentions. It was a mystery to them both, as to who they would end up becoming attached to and they often nervously joked about the possibility of never meeting anyone that either of them even liked well enough to marry, let alone love. It was a fear shared by many of the younger New York females, who had reached their mid-twenties and were still single. Thankfully, these changing times had long since seen the abolishment of families trying to encourage and coerce their daughters into marrying someone of status, or whom they determined as suitable.

Back in Bude, on receiving his first letter from Amelie, written from an address somewhere in New York and received almost three weeks after the Titanic had been lost, Dylan switched from being a reclusive old-looking man, to a vibrant farm labourer again, who was also now the farm's temporary manager. Old Jim, having injured his hand too badly to continue working the farm in the way he used to and feeling desperate to cheer up the grieving Dylan – a lad he had come to look upon as if he were his own son – offered for him to manage the farm, also suggesting Dylan take on a couple of casual hands to help out with the workload. Which had increased dramatically due to the incredible efforts that Dylan had put in over the past few weeks. The older man was thankful of the change in responsibilities and was already seeing the benefits of Dylan's labour on the farm.

The utter relief that consumed Dylan's soul, the moment he saw Amelie's handwriting, was beyond description and as he carefully opened the envelope and read the pages of news inside, tears filled his eyes and rolled down his cheeks.

Despite the letter being addressed to Dylan's home, the postman, having seen the New York date stamp, had rushed over to the farm, knowing Dylan would likely be there. Finding him in the field beside the main entrance, the postman had shouted his name and waving the letter in his hand, called Dylan over. Hopeful of good news, the

Postman was relieved to see Dylan's reaction and turning away himself, with a lump in his own throat, he had left Dylan to privately read the news from America.

Amelie apologised for not writing sooner, explaining how busy life had been and how she had wanted to wait until she had news of a job, before she wrote. Unaware that until this moment, Dylan had assumed she had been lost when the Titanic went down, Amelie described that awful night, how she and Ruby had met and were then saved by Alfie. Continuing on to tell Dylan of Alfie and Mollie, and little William, as well as the fact that she was now living with Ruby and working at the New York Times. As Dylan read the news, his immediate relief at finding out his beloved Amelie was still alive, was mixed with the reminded realisation that he was unlikely to ever see her again. New York sounded like such a fun place for Amelie and she was clearly enjoying her life there. Dylan felt sure that Bude would be the last place she would ever want to be again, not with having so much excitement around her in New York. The newspaper sounded like her perfect dream and he could almost visualise Amelie's happiest of smiles, as she wrote the words to him.

Folding the scented notepaper, Dylan put it to his nose and breathed-in deeply, wanting to smell her touch and feel her energy, his beloved Amelie. As he placed the letter in his waistcoat pocket, Dylan strode back to the farm-house with a lighter step than he had used of late, to tell Jim and Rosie the wonderful news. But as delighted as he was that Amelie was safe, the reminder of her not being there, with him, was still extremely painful and his heart felt torn. Jim and Rosie were delighted for Dylan and hugged him to them as if he were their long-lost son. Suddenly, in that very moment, Dylan realised just how much the two of them meant to him, they truly were like a Mam and Dad, and he felt safe to tell them of his fears at never seeing Amelie again. Sharing that burden, was the best thing that Dylan could have done. Jim and Rosie had guessed that Dylan's pain was about Amelie, but having him open-up and talk to them about it, meant his load was halved and they reassured him, saying he could speak to them about Amelie any time he wanted to, they would always be glad to speak about her. Rosie was especially relieved that Dylan felt able to confide in them and told Jim so, as they cuddled in bed that night, feeling grateful to have each other, whilst feeling Dylan's pain at not having his Amelie.

The weeks were flying by and before the girls knew it, the day had come for their trip across to Wayne County, Michigan, which was, Amelie had been reliably informed, a suburb of Detroit. Ruby's family lived out in the suburbs, having no stomach for city life themselves. Quite why their only daughter had taken it upon herself to travel to the even bigger city of New York, had always puzzled them, but, being good parents, they respected Ruby's life choices, particularly knowing she was being employed by the very respectable Ms Marjorie Madison. That introduction had come about via their friends Henry and Clara Ford, whose grand party in 1911 – to celebrate the sudden growth of their overseas business – had also found Ms Madison on the guest list. Ruby, being the eldest of her parents' children and considered of an appropriate age to be included in society events, had also been invited to join in the fun.

Ruby had always been thankful to Henry and Clara, whom she fondly referred to as Uncle Henry and Aunt Clara. Thanks to their kind invitation and introduction to Aunt Clara's friend, Ms Marjorie Madison, Ruby had become her personal companion and was lucky enough to move to New York, one of the most exciting places she could have thought of. Such had been her excitement at this great opportunity and adventure, Ruby had not considered how difficult she might find being separated from her family for long stretches of time. Whilst the past year had been full of exciting events, including moving into her own apartment and the trip to England, it was only now that Ruby was feeling a strong hankering to go home and see her family. A feeling that had been massively influenced by hers and Amelie's recent brush with death.

With bags packed and feeling extremely excited, the two friends boarded the first train which began their journey from New York to Detroit. Ruby's Papa would meet them at the station in Detroit, using one of Uncle Henry's motor-cars. Amelie was beside herself with excitement at the prospect of travelling in an automobile that actually belonged to Henry Ford himself. This must surely be the start of her article about the man behind the now famous motor-cars. As the two women settled into their carriage, bags safely stowed between the seats, they said hello to their fellow companions and passed the time of day, as one usually does, when meeting a stranger. With the long journey ahead, the two friends soon got chatting on a deeper level to the people sitting with them, one of whom, was a young man, who introduced himself as Bryn Jones and who was also travelling to Detroit, having been told of engineering work being available at the Ford Motor Company. Of course, this revelation triggered much chatter about intriguing co-incidences when Ruby shared her connection to the popular Mr Henry Ford.

Bryn could not believe his luck, as he repeated a saying his Grandma had always remarked upon, *there are no co-*

incidences, just occurrences that are meant to be, to help us all on our journey in this life. Amelie and Ruby could totally relate to that, as they too shared their story of how they first met Alfie on the Titanic, and how he went on to save their lives by getting them into a lifeboat. Then, when they finally reached New York, he had helped Amelie to secure a dream position with the New York Times.

"Your Alfie friend sounds like quite a guy." Bryn already admired this fellow, who had proved his worth by saving two such delightful women, one of whom, Miss Ruby, had captured his full attention, with her twinkling eyes and endearing smile.

Ruby blushed as she felt Bryn's eyes upon her, he was quite a determined chap and she could feel herself being drawn towards him the more he spoke to her. Ruby had never before felt anything quite like it and could feel her heart beating just a little faster. Amelie spotted the immediate spark of attraction and once their journey was well underway, politely withdrew from the conversation, saying she wanted to watch the passing scenery, to see as much of the country as possible.

As the train sped along, Amelie also wondered about her planned meeting with Henry Ford. The rocking motion of the wheels rumbling along the tracks, was oddly soothing and encouraged her to relax, thoughts drifting miles away from the carriage she was travelling in. Amelie's eyes closed and imagining her Caden and their beach in Bude, happy memories flooded her mind, as she watched pictures of Caden in the sunshine; his blond hair and blue eyes seemed so real that she felt as if she were right there with him, laughing at him splashing her with water, as she tried to run away. Caden had always managed to catch her and swing her around, as he pretended to carry her into the water. The images were so real that Amelie's face smiled and her heart glowed with a warmth she had not felt in a long time.

"Be happy my love..." Caden's voice whispered in her ears as the train came to its next stop and Amelie's body jolted back into her seat, her mind suddenly back in the carriage.

Ruby and Bryn were still chatting easily and as the other passengers arose to disembark, the three of them were left alone in the small carriage, until the train pulled off again, slowly building-up speed as it pulled out of the station. Amelie stood up.

"Well, I think I shall go for a walk to stretch my legs and find the buffet-car, would either of you like a drink?

Feeling embarrassed at his own lack of manners, Bryn immediately offered to fetch them all a drink. Smiling, Amelie graciously thanked Bryn, but said she really could do with the walk to wake herself up and besides, she needed to find their sleeper carriage.

"Well, thank you Amelie, perhaps you would at least allow me to pay for the drinks?" Bryn offered Amelie a dollar and suggested getting them some cookies to go with the coffee, if she could manage it all. Feeling sure she could borrow a tray from the buffet-car, Amelie reassured Bryn that she would be fine and suggested he stay and keep Ruby company. To which, Ruby also thanked Amelie and blushed again. Bryn was more than happy to oblige, his liking for Ruby having grown by the minute. Yes, he was very happy to spend time alone with her, wishing he could just lean forward and kiss those rose-bud lips.

As Amelie made her way along the train, she smiled to herself, feeling pleased that Ruby seemed to have met someone she was clearly attracted to and the fact that

Bryn would be living in the same area as her family, really was very convenient indeed. Humming, as she walked, Amelie felt her spirits lift. What an adventure they were on!

Chapter 8

July Fourth

As Amelie and Ruby's final train pulled into Detroit, Bryn and Ruby, having already exchanged addresses, confirmed their arrangement to meet on the Saturday afternoon. Amelie, having already reassured Ruby that she would be fine on her own for an afternoon, could see that the two of them were smitten with each other. An unexpected happening, but one that Amelie was happy about, for Ruby especially. This Bryn chap seemed like such a nice man and he reminded her somewhat of Dylan, being similar in build, with dark hair, also coming across as very dependable and likeable.

Feeling extremely grateful for Amelie's understanding and agreement to amuse herself whilst Ruby met-up with Bryn on Saturday afternoon, Ruby silently mouthed a thank you at her friend. Knowing her family were always very accommodating, Ruby also felt certain they would be happy to entertain Amelie, whilst she, Ruby, was out of the house for a few hours. Besides which, her parents would be overjoyed to discover she had finally met a man that she felt attracted to. Ruby had no doubts that they would welcome Bryn with open arms.

Wanting to spend a few more minutes with her, Bryn offered to carry Ruby's bag off the train, which caused her to blush as she thanked him, adding that her Papa would be waiting to help them with their luggage. The moment the three of them disembarked from the train, Ruby's eyes were scanning for her Papa and sure enough, there he was. Forgetting her manners, Ruby abandoned her friends and immediately ran into his arms, and as he caught her, he swirled her around.

"Ruby, my darling girl, you don't know how good it is to see you again!"

No words could describe how lucky Mike Carter felt at seeing his daughter alive and well. They had all been beside themselves with despair, until the moment Ruby's message had arrived, informing them of her survival.

"Papa, it is so good to see you, how is Mama and the boys?" Ruby was giddy with excitement and thrilled to hear that all was well at home. As Amelie and Bryn caught up with them, Ruby's face lit up again and she turned to introduce them.

"Papa, this is my dear friend Amelie."

As Amelie stepped forward the older man opened his arms to welcome her into their family, immediately thanking her for being such a good friend to Ruby.

"It is I who should thank Ruby, Mr Carter, she has been an angel in helping me to settle into New York life." Accepting his welcome hug, Amelie continued with her greeting, "It is so lovely to finally meet you and I would like to thank you for your generous invitation for me to join such an important family weekend." Amelie warmed to Ruby's Papa immediately, not realising until that moment, quite how much she had missed her own Father's embrace. Losing both of her parents at the same time, had been the hardest thing and Amelie had been so glad that Caden was there to support her during that time of immense grief.

"You're very welcome Amelie, we are delighted to have you join us." Seeing Bryn holding Ruby's bag, Mike Carter begged a question, "So, who is this young man then?" Turning to properly face Bryn, who had patiently watched and waited as this family scene unfolded in front of him, Mike assessed the young man standing before him.

Ruby had never blushed so much in one day as she introduced Bryn, "Papa, this is Bryn, we met on the train, he is hoping to find work at Uncle Henry's factory and has been very good company for both Amelie and I. Also, he's completely new to town, so, I agreed to show him around a bit on Saturday afternoon." Ruby was very forthright, which appealed to Bryn. For Mike, it was exactly the type of behaviour that he now expected from his proud and headstrong daughter.

"Well, new to town eh, Bryn, so, I'm guessing you've not made any plans as yet? Other than for Saturday afternoon of course…" Mike winked at his daughter as he reached out and shook the younger man's hand firmly, before continuing with another invitation. "Well now, it just so happens that we do have some free positions in the factory. So, if you'd like to come along on Friday afternoon, we can talk through your experience." Mike watched the surprised delight in the younger man's face and before he had a chance to reply, asked another question, "So, where are you staying tonight?" Mike could see his daughter's eyes shining, so he guessed this chap was someone special to her.

"Wow, well, first off, hello Mr Carter, Sir, it's very nice to meet you and well, Friday would be fantastic, thank you, would two o'clock be a good time?" Referring to the unexpected offer of an informal interview and feeling surprised to find himself in this situation, Bryn was almost gushing as he spoke, "As for tonight, I was going to look for a boarding-house in town.

"Nay lad, there's no need for that, there's a guest house a short distance from where we live, I'll drop you there and you can come on over to join us for dinner this evening. If you don't already have plans, that is?" Mike was feeling generous and knowing his wife Edie always cooked enough food to feed an army, one extra mouth at the table would be no problem to her. Besides, watching Ruby's face light-up at his suggestion, was all the thanks Mike needed. Wrapping an arm around his daughter as he took her bag from Bryn, Mike accepted the younger man's shocked thanks and grinned at him, seeing he was completely gobsmacked, but very happy at Mike's generous offer.

The four of them started walking towards the motor-car. It was a comfortable, if not somewhat unusual situation for both Bryn and Amelie. The two of them exchanged knowing smiles, as they walked behind, watching and listening to the excited chatter between Ruby and her Papa, as the four of them crossed the station forecourt.

Approaching the motor-car, like Amelie, Bryn was very impressed, "Wow, this is fantastic Mr Carter."

Mike glowed, he was always proud of the motor-cars that he helped Henry Ford design and thanked Bryn for the compliment. As the younger man reached down to help load all of their bags onto the back of it, Ruby and Amelie settled themselves into the rear seats. Bryn thanked Mike again for his generosity.

"Bryn lad, no need to thank me again, if we can't help one another out now and then, it would be a sorry old world now, wouldn't it?"

It was a statement rather than an actual question because Mike knew he liked Bryn already, but also being no fool and generally a good judge of character, inviting young Bryn to join them for dinner proved to be a useful arrangement for them both. Mike could reserve his full judgement as to whether Bryn was suitable to date his

Ruby, until the after-dinner questioning took place. Bryn on the other hand, who had expected Ruby's family to grill him, was feeling a little apprehensive, but knowing how keen he already felt about Ruby, he also knew it would be an inevitable process and so he welcomed it.

Driving home was exhilarating for them all, the motor-car was a joy and all of them loved the journey, not wanting it to end, whilst simultaneously feeling excited to get on with their July fourth celebrations.

As Mike dropped Bryn at the guest-house, he explained how to get to the Carter family home for later and suggested he ask Mabel, the owner of the guest-house, to loan him a bicycle, saying Mike Carter had asked the favour. The guest-house had three old family bicycles in the shed, which Mable often loaned-out to her trusted paying-guests, thinking of it as a helping-hand for them.

Waving goodbye to Ruby, as the motor-car drove away, Bryn turned and walked towards the colonial style guest-house. It looked well-kept and very welcoming with its front porch swept clean, and cushioned chairs arranged comfortably, allowing the resident guests some outside space in which to enjoy the evening sun. Having checked Bryn into one of her front bedrooms, Mabel was only too pleased to accommodate Mike's suggestion and asked Bryn to also thank Mike for bringing him to her guest-house.

He's a darling, that one – is how Mable felt about Mike, who was always helping her out with extra guests, most, invariably having business at the Ford factory.

Mabel also immediately took to the young Bryn, who seemed like a good sort.

Having paid Mabel a week in advance, Bryn quickly unpacked his things and freshened up. If he could impress Mike well enough, he was certain that he would be successful in finding work at the Ford motor factory, thereby needing to extend his stay with Mabel and be close to Ruby.

When the motor-car pulled up outside Ruby's family home, her Mama and brothers rushed out to meet her. They had missed Ruby so much and having thought she had been lost at sea, were all feeling even more emotional than normal. Ruby rushed towards them, accepting all the hugs, kisses and brotherly jibes at being away from home for far too long.

Amelie felt a very slight pang of envy as she watched this happy scene. Mike, glancing at Amelie and sensing her feelings, put a fatherly arm around her shoulders and slowly walked her towards his family.

"Come on now, you lot, put Ruby down and come and meet her lovely friend, Amelie." Happily introducing them, as each turned towards Amelie and stepped forward to offer smiles, a hug from Edie, who looked just as homely as Amelie had imagined and hand-shakes from the boys.

"So, here then Amelie, this is Edie, my wonderful wife..." Mike winked at Edie as he said that, "Then there's Frank, our oldest boy, Peter, the middle one and John, who's the youngest."

"Aww, Pa, I'm not that young now." John always felt embarrassed at being referred to as the youngest, when in fact all three boys were grown men.

Of course, to Mike and Edie, they were always going to be their little boys, just as Ruby was and always would be, their little girl. After Frank and Peter had welcomed Amelie to the family, they went off to fetch hers and Ruby's luggage from the motor-car.

Edie ushered Ruby and Amelie inside, with Mike following behind, feeling proud and delighted to have them all together for this special weekend. Mike had missed Ruby just as much as his wife and sons had, so to have her home safe and sound, with her lovely friend, made him very happy.

Edie had been baking for the past two days, spending almost as much time cleaning flour from her hands, aprons and kitchen, as she did loading and unloading trays of pies, cakes and pastries from the oven. Now, laid out on the table were more cakes and pastries than Amelie had seen in a long time, other than in the window of their local bakery and as the family tucked into them with much appreciation, Amelie marvelled at them all. Their familiar and comfortable family-love was obvious for all to see and certainly was beyond any reproach. As Amelie chose a piece of pecan pie, much to Edie's delight, she complimented the delicious taste and lightness of the pastry. Edie was always grateful for any compliment of her cooking and glowed with pride, thanking Amelie and feeling very happy to have pleased Ruby's friend so easily.

Once bellies were filled and the table was being cleared, Edie suggested Ruby show Amelie to the room she would be using, so she could unpack her bag and freshen-up. It was actually Frank's bedroom, which he had offered-up voluntarily, suggesting he share with John who, somehow, over the years, had ended up with the biggest bedroom. With fresh linen on the bed and clean towels provided, Amelie was thrilled at the comfort of her room and thanked Frank for generously giving it up. Frank, who had not taken his eyes off of Amelie since she first stepped out of the car, was delighted to think she would be sleeping in his bed and answered immediately.

"Oh, it's no trouble at all Amelie, in fact it's my pleasure." Frank smiled broadly at Amelie, as he left her to unpack and freshen-up, causing her to smile at his retreating back.

Ruby, having already pointed out where the bathroom was whilst showing Amelie around the house, winked at Amelie and left her alone, as she disappeared into her own bedroom. Frank's comment, which, even though the others had not heard it, had not been lost on Ruby and she smiled to herself, certain that her eldest brother was smitten with her new friend. The thought pleased Ruby no end, Frank was a very decent man, and yes, because he was her brother, she could be accused of bias, but Frank had always been far more sensible than his years and was a sensitive, yet very capable chap. Amelie would be a fabulous match for him, being undeniably beautiful, yet also strong and capable, clever, and very funny. Ruby's match-making mind began to race, until she remembered Caden. Hmmm, would Amelie be open to meeting someone else yet? Ruby wasn't totally convinced and decided she would take Frank to one side, to privately explain the situation. She didn't want him to put his foot in it by speaking out of turn at the wrong moment, or anything like that.

Amelie really did feel very grateful to Frank for giving up his room and as she stared at a photo of him holding a baseball trophy, which was stood on his dresser, he suddenly seemed very familiar to her. There was something about him that she couldn't quite put her finger on. It wasn't as if he reminded her of Caden, because Frank had light brown hair, whilst Caden had been blond, and he was stockier than Caden, but those blue eyes, and his smile… Amelie puzzled over that, as she unpacked her things and hung them up on the back of the door.

Using the bathroom to freshen-up, she decided to change into different clothes; feeling the need to make an effort to look more presentable after their long train journey. Ruby had been a complete darling in familiarising Amelie with the house and so, she only felt a tiny bit out of place at being in this very welcoming and loving family home. Thinking how lucky Ruby was to have such a lovely family, Amelie genuinely felt a warmth for them all. The whole family had welcomed her as if she were one of their own and she was very happy to find that like Ruby, they were all very normal people. Yes, a delightfully normal family, with no airs or put-on graces and no awkwardness. Amelie imagined what a fabulous weekend they would all have together.

The afternoon seemed to fly by, as the excited chatter grew and the expected re-telling of their Titanic experience was relayed. Everyone was enthralled, if not a little anxious at the closeness of the event having a very different ending for them all. With the story told and not wanting to leave everyone feeling depressed, Amelie reminded Ruby to tell her family of her new promotion with Ms Madison. As Ruby did so, the chatter and congratulations moved on and the air buzzed with more laughter.

Leaving Ruby with her Papa and brother's, Amelie offered to help Edie in the kitchen. Dinner was almost ready and her offer to help resulted in the two of them laying the table together. As they did so, Edie asked Amelie a little about herself, saying that Ruby had briefly told her of Amelie's loss, for which Edie offered her condolences. Not wanting to upset her guest, Edie also explained that she didn't want to pry, but if Amelie ever needed an ear, she was there for her.

What a sweet thing to say. Amelie thanked Edie for her kind thoughts and said she didn't mind talking about Caden and would tell Edie more about him over the weekend. Amelie didn't want to spoil this happy family day by sharing her sad story.

The two women fell into a comfortable conversation and Edie, understanding Amelie's reasoning, was grateful to her, for considering their feelings as she again remarked upon how thankful they all were to have young Ruby home. Edie asked Amelie about her impression of Bryn, the young man who was expected to be joining them for dinner and who, Mike had told her, Ruby seemed to have a very soft spot for. Amelie gladly gave up her thoughts and impressions of Bryn, having taken him on face value since the moment they both met him. She was happy for Ruby and said her first impressions were good and that Bryn seemed like a very decent person. Laughing with Edie, Amelie also said she was quite looking forward to the 'family grilling' he would no doubt get later. Laughing easily together, the two women agreed he was brave to have accepted Mike's invitation so willingly, which was also considered to be a good sign to them. Young Bryn must truly like Ruby to agree to meeting her whole family on such a special day.

The dinner was almost ready by the time Bryn arrived and after Ruby had greeted him, the men took over the conversation, offering to show him around the town and familiarise him with where all the important places were.

Leaving Bryn to the inevitable questions about work, that she knew her brothers would ask, Ruby disappeared to fetch him a drink and to let her Mama, and Amelie know of his arrival. The two women followed her back outside and rescued Bryn from the initial onslaught of questions, with Edie laughing and excusing the boys for being so forthright. But Bryn was fine, he had expected it and said as much to Edie, as she welcomed him to their family home.

"It really is my pleasure to be here Mrs Carter and I would like to thank you and Mr… err, Mike, for your very kind invitation." Bryn remembered Mike's previous instruction and grinned at him as Ruby's Papa replied before Edie had a chance to.

"That's fine my boy, now, tell us all about your family and where you are from."

Edie, not minding that Mike had jumped-in, was glad to return to the kitchen, not wanting their food to spoil, although, also not before asking Bryn to save telling that part of his story until they were all seated around the table, because she too wanted to hear more about him.

"Perhaps you and Mike can talk motor-cars whilst you're waiting to eat?" Edie suggested, knowing that would trigger immediate chatter, as she retreated to the kitchen, asking Ruby and Amelie to help her serve. Which basically meant, filling various bowls with potatoes and vegetables, then placing them down the centre of the table, along with a plate of three different types of meat, for everyone to help themselves to. Ruby added jugs of gravy to the table, whilst Frank poured out glasses of home-made lemonade for everyone.

With the family and new friends gathered around the table, dinner was a lively and very happy affair, with all of them learning more about Bryn.

When it got around to Amelie's turn to share her story, Frank's eyes never moved from her face; he was enthralled to know everything about her and to just watch her, as she smiled and shared a little of herself. It was a magical moment for him.

Just as much as Frank watched Amelie, so Bryn also watched Ruby, catching her eye whenever nobody was looking and quietly mouthing to her that she looked beautiful. It was as if love were in the air and angel dust had been sprinkled over them all, such was the good humour and laughter that they all shared and enjoyed. Mike and Edie glowed with pride and great happiness, both feeling overjoyed to have their house full again and to see their grown-children, and new friends happily chatting together.

As dinner came to a natural end and seeing the brothers picking up empty dishes, Bryn also offered to help clear the table, thanking Edie for their delicious meal. Mike invited Amelie out to the front porch to talk business, as he also explained that in this family, everyone was taught to help with household chores.

Edie and Mike believed that all of their children should grow-up being able to live independently, no matter whether they were male or female. It was a good family tradition to have. Mike laughed, saying it was a tradition the boys now appreciated much more than they had when they were younger. Realising that along with the practicality of it, helping-out seemed to impress the girls, which Mike also advised, was a very useful addition to their toolbox of life-skills. Amelie agreed, enjoying the good humour Mike instilled in his approach to setting down the house-rules for his boys.

"So, Amelie, Ruby tells me you were hoping to run a story about Henry and his latest success on the international market?" Mike cut straight to the point, knowing the reporter in Amelie would appreciate his candour.

"Yes, Mr Carter... sorry, Mike." Laughing as Ruby's Papa reminded her to call him Mike, Amelie continued, "I was thinking that if we could share a story about the man behind the motor-cars, it might add a different level of interest and appeal to the smaller business market, as well as the international one, which I understand is expanding rapidly at the moment."

Amelie had done her research and was hopeful that Mike would be happy to support her idea, and offer an introduction to Henry Ford.

"Well Amelie, that sounds like a fine idea, I can see where you're coming from and I reckon Henry would be glad to give you an interview. Besides, to have an article in the New York Times would be a real bonus and he'll certainly appreciate the free advertising."

Mike was quite excited at the prospects this article could hold for his closest friend and business partner. Whilst not *officially* regarded as a partner in the firm, Henry always referred to Mike as such, because he was his reliable right-hand man and Mike shared Henry's enthusiasm for new ideas. Because of that closeness, Henry had always rewarded Mike very well for his commitment and help in growing the business, and in fact, unbeknown to Mike, Henry was about to gift-him the motor-car he had loaned to Mike for the weekend, to thank him for helping get their international business moving so strongly. It was an exceptionally generous gift, but one that Henry felt Mike had more than earned over the years.

Mike suggested to Amelie that he would speak to Henry on Friday and see if they couldn't arrange a few hours to talk, sometime over the holiday weekend, knowing that Henry would be at home for the whole weekend because Clara's father was staying with them. Mike also knew that Clara wouldn't mind, she was a fine woman who had always supported Henry, whenever he needed to take a bit of time-out from the family to deal with some aspect of the business. It was partly the reason that the Ford motor business was as successful as it was, Clara's undying support was certainly Henry's most valuable asset. Mike also guessed that Clara would encourage Henry to take-up the very welcome advertising opportunity that Amelie would be offering.

Amelie thanked Mike again and told him she would never forget this weekend, or his wonderful support in helping her to achieve further success. As they hugged again, Mike suggested they both get back inside to join the others.

Chapter 9

Henry and Clara

When Mike explained Amelie's suggestion to Henry, he was indeed very keen for the idea and as expected, agreed to speak to Amelie on the Saturday afternoon, which coincided beautifully with Ruby's plans to be out with Bryn. Henry also suggested that Mike come along with Edie and take tea with them all, by way of also celebrating the fourth of July weekend together, adding, "It'll please Clara's father no end, to be able to say that not only has he met a New York Times Reporter, but one who also survived the sinking of the Titanic!"

Mike, knowing Clara's father well, agreed with Henry and felt sure the elder gentleman would have much to ask Amelie, thereby keeping her entertained too.

As the two men continued their working day, Mike mentioned to Henry that he was interviewing a young man that Ruby had met on the train, who, coincidentally, was looking for engineering work. Henry was pleased to hear this news, knowing their local supply of engineering talent was pretty much running out, with most young men already engaged at the factory and more needed to support their ever-expanding business. Wishing Mike good luck with the interview, Henry winked and said he might pop his head around the door to meet the young man that had caught Ruby's eye. Mike nodded agreeably, "Good idea Henry, I'll send word once he arrives." Henry had always kept a watchful eye over young Ruby, she was like the daughter he never had. Ruby was very precious to both himself and his wife, Clara.

Bryn arrived promptly and made a point of being friendly to the receptionist, knowing that lots of people often overlooked them. Many potential employees not realising that they were often the very people who advised the hiring manager of how, as a prospective candidate, they had behaved in reception, including which questions, if any, were asked and with what demeanour.

Even with potential barriers already broken down, following their chat the previous day and half the questions already answered, Bryn was still very keen to impress Mike; he was dressed very smartly and felt fully prepared for whatever question Mike might throw at him. As with any other business situation, Bryn expected a fairly formal discussion.

As it happened, Mike felt relaxed enough with Bryn to run the interview informally, having already established that his interest lay in the mechanics of the engine, rather than the bodywork. Mike had already decided he was happy to take the young man on and just wanted to work through which parts of the engine Bryn was most interested in making. Being a forward-thinking man, whenever he could and generally for the first six months, Mike liked to allocate his staff to work on the parts of the motor-cars they were most interested in, realising it would keep them enthusiastic and motivated. After the six months, he tended to then start moving them around on a rota, so they got to see how the whole car was built. For those who had no preference, he allowed the needs of the business to dictate allocation. That said, anyone who was not enjoying their work, could ask to be moved, such was the flexible nature of the culture that Mike and Henry both liked to promote, having enough personal experience under their belts, to realise what worked well for them and helped drive the success of the business.

Just before the end of the hour that Mike had allocated for his chat to Bryn, Henry popped his head around the door and seeing that Bryn was still there, walked-in to say hello properly.

"So, young man, Mike has told me some good things about you and no doubt, told you lots about how we work here." Moving to shake Bryn's hand, he introduced himself, "I'm Henry and I understand you're Bryn Jones, a new beau of young Ruby's." Henry grinned at the younger man, immediately putting him at ease with his unusually casual approach.

"Yes, I am and yes, I would very much like to become Ruby's beau..." feeling ever so slightly embarrassed, Bryn glanced quickly at a grinning Mike before looking back to Henry, "...and thank you Sir, Mr Ford, I truly appreciate you giving me this opportunity and I won't let you down." Bryn was almost tripping over his own words in his eagerness to please his new employers. Henry, seeing a little of himself in the lad, accepted his thanks and told him, that as long as he turned up every day and worked hard, they would all get along just fine.

With that, Henry left them to it, giving Mike the nod that he was happy with Bryn, as he walked out the door, "I'll catch you later Mike, lots to catch up with before the weekend arrives," and with that, Henry Ford was gone. Bryn's shoulders visibly relaxed.

Advising him of what time to arrive on Monday, Mike explained that he would take Bryn through the workshops himself and introduce him to the foreman, who would show Bryn where he would be working and how to operate the machinery.

Bryn couldn't thank Mike enough and as the two parted, he said so again, both about the job, and more importantly, Mike's obvious approval of him courting the lovely Ruby.

Feeling as if he were walking on air, Bryn made his way back to the guest-house, to confirm to Mable that he would indeed be staying on for at least a month, or until he found somewhere a little more permanent. Relieved and quite overwhelmed at being sorted, both in terms of somewhere to stay *and* having secured a job, also now having Mike's blessing to court Ruby, meant Bryn was bursting to tell her everything. Borrowing the bicycle from Mable again, Bryn cycled the two miles to Ruby's house, knowing the boys would all be working, but expecting she would be home with her Mama and Amelie.

Sure enough, as he reached the house, Bryn could hear the women's laughter coming out through the open windows. What a joy that was to him. Already smiling, he propped the bicycle up against the fence and rushed towards the front porch, only to be startled by Ruby opening the door at the very moment he reached the top step. A pure coincidence, it was one which pleased Ruby immensely at finding Bryn on their front porch and as she stepped out, he grinned at her, telling her he had the most wonderful news that just couldn't wait until tomorrow, so he had rushed over to share it with her. Hearing Bryn's voice, Edie and Amelie waited a few moments before following Ruby out to greet him, and feeling pleased for Ruby, both women congratulated Bryn on hearing his exciting news. Edie was particularly thrilled that Bryn had felt so inclined to rush over and tell her daughter the exciting news. This was another good sign in her book and Edie hoped that Ruby would appreciate what that meant. Stepping forward to hug Bryn and take the flower-cutting scissors from Ruby's hand, so that she too could hug Bryn, Edie and Amelie, then left them to each other and went down into the garden to cut some flowers for the table. Both feeling happy at the keenness of Ruby's new beau.

When Mike returned that evening, he told Edie and Amelie about Henry's invitation for tea with the family the following day, and confirmed to Amelie that whilst they were there, Henry would be happy to talk with her for the article she had suggested. Amelie beamed and having been warned about the many questions Clara's father would also ask, she laughed a little nervously as she thanked Mike again. Amelie was always happy to ask and answer questions, but she had become a little more guarded about her personal life, since starting at the paper.

Their evening was again, one of happy laughter and enjoyment as the family, and Amelie, sat down over dinner and talked about the events of their day. Peter and John didn't have much news as such, other than to report they had decided to get up very early the next morning, to show Bryn a bit of town before he met Ruby for the afternoon. Both were keen to befriend Bryn, feeling hopeful he might bring their sister home to them, but also because they quite liked him and thought he would make a great addition to their family. Frank's day was no different to normal, but he did also state he would wax the motor-car in the morning, before Mike returned it to Henry in the afternoon. An offer which was triggered more by the desire to spend his spare time around the house, close to Amelie, rather than any desperate need to get covered in wax all morning.

As it happened, unbeknown to him, Frank did get his chance to impress Amelie that morning, when she casually glanced out of the window, only to witness his muscular arms and back, clearly visible through the thin fabric of his shirt, as he was reaching across the motor-car bonnet, waxing it until the paintwork glistened in the sunshine. Amelie again felt immediately impressed by Frank and that uncanny familiarity, which had come over her the day she arrived, had not left her. Amelie found herself absent-mindedly fantasising for a brief moment about what Frank would look like with his shirt off.

Edie, who caught sight of Amelie watching Frank and having already spotted the attraction between her eldest son and Ruby's new best friend, glowed inside, thinking how marvellous it would be for the two of them to get together. Until, remembering Caden, Edie's hopes sank again, just a little, knowing that Amelie would likely still be grieving for her husband and that Frank would have to be patient if he wanted to win this one's heart. Wanting to explore that scenario a little, but without wanting to pry too much, Edie decided to broach the subject with Amelie.

"Amelie, sweetheart, I have been wondering about your Caden and how you are coping now that two years have passed?"

"To be honest with you Edie, most of the time, I am fine, but occasionally I still have a bad day, which is often triggered by other emotional events. Yesterday was a bit like that, although I was enjoying having a truly wonderful family day with you all, I did also wonder what my own children would have been like, had Caden and I been able to have a family."

Feeling comfortable with Edie, Amelie began to share her true feelings. The two women found themselves subconsciously bonding over their discussion about Caden and his loving ways, his unquestionable bravery and of course, his ultimate sacrifice at helping someone in need. Edie could see that Amelie's love for Caden had been huge, but she felt sure that Caden would want his beloved wife to continue her life being happy. Taking the bull by the horns, Edie suggested that perhaps Amelie *should* allow herself to find love again.

Despite her keenness to match-make her Frank with Amelie, Edie's advice was completely genuine, because whilst she would dearly love to see Amelie and Frank get together, Edie was truly concerned about Amelie allowing herself to be happy again. If that happiness included her Frank, so much the better, but in this moment, Amelie's future happiness was as important to Edie as if she were her own daughter.

Bursting in through the doorway and unknowingly interrupting their moment of bonding, Mike suggested they'd best make tracks over to Henry and Clara's, so as not to be late for afternoon tea. Knowing Clara's delicious cakes only too well, Mike didn't want to miss out on tasting her latest creation.

As the three of them walked outside, it struck Amelie that Frank had done an amazing job of waxing the motor-car and she was still admiring the bodywork gleaming in the sunshine, as he offered her his hand, simultaneously opening the rear passenger door, so she could step in and take a seat. Amelie thanked Frank and attracted again by his familiar blue eyes, smiled at him. Wishing her good luck for the chat with Uncle Henry, Frank beamed at Amelie and added that he very much looked forward to seeing her that evening. As Amelie smiled at him again, so Frank's heart was completely and permanently captured by her very being. Amelie was a woman to love and he was certain that one day, he would marry her.

Mike checked everyone was ready and started the engine, feeling very content with how the long weekend was going so far; everyone seemed relaxed and comfortable with each other, which made him happy. Smiling at Edie as he pulled away, the threesome started their journey into Detroit. It was quite a treat for Amelie and although the noise of the motor made it a little tricky for her to hear them every time, Amelie appreciated Edie and Mike's efforts to inform her of the many interesting sights along the way.

As they journeyed into the city, Amelie found herself hankering for the peace of the family home they had just come from and her home-town of Bude. It was an unexpected and strange sensation to find herself not wanting to be in the city, especially having started her new life in the even bigger city of New York. Feeling slightly uneasy, Amelie kept her feelings quiet and distracted herself with thoughts about her pitch to Henry. Already feeling a familiarity with Henry Ford, due to the family connections, Amelie felt quite calm about meeting the great man himself. It was just being back in the city that somehow unnerved her. Perhaps talking about Caden this morning, had been the trigger?

As they reached the Ford's house, Amelie tried to shake off the unwelcome feelings that were invading her mind. Happy to be meeting Henry and Clara Ford, Amelie was not surprised to find they were delightful people, clearly very much shaped by their success, but not at all pretentious. At least, not with her. This was a good start and Amelie's mind immediately began mentally writing their story, as they welcomed her, introducing their Son, Edsel and Clara's Father, Mr Melvin Bryant. Both Henry and Clara remarked on how lovely it was to meet one of young Ruby's friends, who was also a reporter and how her wish to write about their company was such an unexpected pleasure, that they very much looked forward to hearing more about her life too. Instinctively, Amelie

109

knew she would keep any talk of herself to a minimum, to be sure she had sufficient time to question Henry and Clara, and gain enough information for her article about the Ford's. As it turned out, Amelie need not have been concerned, Henry and Clara were very open and willing to talk about themselves, and their business.

However, like Ruby's family, they too wished to hear all about Amelie and Ruby's experience on the Titanic. Clara's father, having read several articles on the subject already and keeping a watchful eye on the legal aspects of the many claims being made against the owners, was especially keen to hear everything. Amelie was willing to oblige, but longed for the day when nobody asked her again. Re-living that awful night was still traumatic for her and she just wanted to leave it all behind.

The remainder of the afternoon was very enjoyable though and as they left for the journey home, Amelie thanked both Clara for her hospitality and Henry for being so candid with her, promising to let him know which edition the article would be printed in. Henry Ford had given Amelie his personal telephone number, so she could do just that. Feeling quite honoured, Amelie had folded the piece of paper carefully and placed it safely in her purse.

The highlight of the afternoon turned out not to be the interview for the newspaper though, instead, Henry had taken the opportunity of telling Mike, that the motor-car was now his to keep, as a thank you for all the hard work and effort he had given over their years of working together, helping build the business into the successful company that it now was. Mike was totally overwhelmed by Henry's most generous of offers, as was Edie, both of them saying it was too much. But both Henry and Clara insisted, knowing that having a motor-car would be a massive help to their friends and besides, Henry joked, it would encourage their boys to keep up their own dreams of owning one.

What a revelation this trip was turning out to be! Amelie was impressed by the strength of friendships and families here, whilst feeling immensely grateful to be a part of the comforting warmth that she felt around Mike and Edie's family, and friends.

By the time they returned home, Mike and Edie were bursting to tell the family all about Uncle Henry's generous gift and laughed as the boys pleaded with Mike to be able to have a go at driving it, now that Mike owned the shiny motor-car. Mike had known his boys would be wanting to have a turn and promised each of them, he would teach them to drive, reminding them they could only use the motor with his permission. All three of his sons nodded their understanding and then grinned at each other, this July fourth weekend was one none of them would ever forget!

Ruby had arrived home before her parents and taken the opportunity to talk privately to Frank, who, on hearing about Caden, felt as though the bottom of his world had dropped out. But, with Ruby's encouraging reminder that it would just take a bit more time to win Amelie's heart, Frank's spirits lifted and he told Ruby, that no matter what, he would wait, such was the depth of his feelings towards the very intriguing Amelie.

Chapter 10

Returning to New York

When the unavoidable time arrived for Ruby and Amelie to begin their journey back to New York, neither felt inclined to go. For Ruby, it meant leaving behind her family, as well as her lovely Bryn and despite promises of writing to each other to continue their courtship, she knew she would miss him like crazy. Like she had for him, Bryn had already stolen Ruby's heart on the journey from New York.

As for Amelie, it was the closeness of having a happy family around her, that she would miss the most. Edie and Mike had been so kind and welcoming, as had the boys, although, she expected that Frank would likely be secretly glad to have his room back. Having a family like Ruby did, meant knowing you have people there to catch you if you fall and Amelie knew she would miss them all terribly.

Encouraging his daughter to hurry, Mike reminded Ruby of the long train journey ahead and with hugs given, and final goodbye kisses shared, he started-up the engine. Frank had been tempted to go with them, but wavering, he eventually decided not to, feeling concerned that he may give the game away over his feelings for Amelie and frighten her off. But when Mike suggested Frank hop in to keep him company on the journey home, all those worries disappeared and Frank jumped at the chance to say goodbye to Amelie again. Edie smiled at her son, knowing he was smitten as, and waving goodbye to the girls, she called out to them to visit again as soon as they could.

The journey back to New York seemed so much quicker than the trip out, that it felt like no time at all before Ruby and Amelie were back in their apartment, unpacking bags and hanging up the clothes that Edie had insisted on washing for them, to save them the trouble when they got back. Their excited chatter about everything that had happened during their trip and the new romance developing between Ruby and Bryn, which in truth, had dominated the conversation, had left them both thankful for their lovely break. If not a little exhausted, from all the travelling. Freshly bathed and ready for bed, Ruby dared to broach the subject of Frank and how lovely it had been of him to give up his room for Amelie, who agreed, as, imagining herself getting into his bed again instead of her own, she continued sharing her thoughts about him.

"Ruby, he is such a lovely man, you're so lucky to have him as a brother and I can see why you are so proud of him, well, of them all, actually. Your family are amazing and I'm just so happy that we met and that you invited me to join you all." Amelie paused contentedly before continuing, "Ruby, you don't know what it has meant to me, to be a part of your family for the past few days. I'm quite at a loss as to how we will manage without them all." Amelie was feeling a little emotional, she supposed that was due to being over-tired, until Ruby admitted she felt the same.

"You're right Amelie, it's been so wonderful being with the family again, I didn't realise how much I had missed them all, but I too am so glad we met and I'm really happy that you came with me. My family love you." The two friends hugged for the longest moment before wishing each other a good night's sleep.

Lying in the dark, Amelie thought about Frank and

tried to recall all the lovely smells of that wonderful house, as she silently wished them all good-night, imagining she was back there with them.

From her own bed, Ruby was sending love and prayers to her family, and to her lovely Bryn, before she too drifted off to sleep.

Both women slept with happy thoughts in their heads and love in their heart's, until their morning alarm rang out, causing both Amelie and Ruby to groan, surely it couldn't be morning already, could it? Dragging themselves out of bed, they went about their usual routine before leaving for a day of work, with agreements made on who would be picking up which groceries on their way home later.

Back into their normal routines, Ruby was keen to catch-up with Ms Madison's diary arrangements and of course Amelie, had her amazing Henry Ford article to write-up for Stan and Bob to review, which she hoped they would approve for print.

Back in the office, Amelie was keen to strike whilst the iron was hot and tapped away at an almost furious pace, hoping to get approval for immediate inclusion in one of that week's editions.

Meanwhile, Ms Madison was overjoyed to see Ruby and asked her all about her family visit. Of course, as expected, Ruby was unable to hold back her enthusiasm about their trip back home and gave a full account of every day, including that she had met a fine young man on the train out of New York and, who now lived in her home town.

Feeling a little tug of envy at Ruby's visit to the familiar suburbs that Marjorie Madison had also grown-up in, she surprised Ruby by stating that she would rather have been there herself too, instead of being stuck here in the city. A sharing of feelings which very much took Ruby by surprise, Marjorie Madison went on to add that whilst the city had many benefits, the likes of which, she had taken great advantage of over the years, their recent experience on the Titanic, had caused her to re-think her priorities. Whilst Ruby had been away, Marjorie had come up with a new plan for her future, which she was keen to speak to her young protégé about. This new idea had been keeping Marjorie Madison's mind fully occupied and she was relieved that Ruby was finally back, to hear her idea and hopefully, concur with the proposal for Ruby to join her.

"Ruby, it is so good to have you back and to hear all the stories of home. I am so pleased that you have met Bryn, he sounds like a fine, young man."

Ruby felt a little surprised at Ms Madison's excited mood, particularly as she seemed to be bursting with anticipated excitement. Unable to wait any longer, Marjorie Madison shared her thoughts.

"Ruby, how would you feel about becoming my long-term companion and moving back to Detroit with me?"

Marjorie Madison had been quite worried that Ruby would not want to leave New York, but on hearing of her new beau, she supposed that Ruby might now actually be quite happy at the idea of moving closer to home. There was to be the promise of a small, paid-for house, but with the request that Ruby be on-call for all events and distance travelling, with the option of paid time-off to the equivalent of two weeks of the year. Of course, the daily working and managing her diary, would remain the same, Marjorie explained, but for now, that was her offer and she hoped Ruby would accept it.

Well, Ruby's chin almost hit the floor, she could not believe this almost perfect offer. It would mean that she could live closer to her family and of course, to Bryn. In fact, the offer sounded almost too good to be true and Ruby jumped at the idea.

"Oh, Ms Madison, that sounds wonderful. I'm overwhelmed, the timing couldn't have been more perfect. What with me having met my lovely Bryn..."

Ruby realised she was so excited that her words were almost tripping her up and so she just hugged her employer in the most unexpected way.

Marjorie Madison was touched and VERY happy that Ruby had accepted her offer so quickly, without even wanting to take time to think about it. Explaining that it would take time for the house to be sold in New York, but that she would keep Ruby's apartment on, so that the two of them had somewhere to stay, whenever they came into town. Marjorie did still have a busy social life to contend with and so, she had decided she would need a base in both places. But, as the property was far cheaper around Detroit, there would be no problem with finding something suitable for both herself and her unborn baby, and Ruby, by using the proceeds of her extremely large New York house.

"Oh, that's wonderful. Yes, that's perfect. Let's say it's all settled then. We shall start making arrangements immediately and if all goes according to plan, we will both be spending Christmas in our new homes and this little one..." Marjorie placed a hand on her swollen tummy, "...will have arrived and be the best present I could ever have." Marjorie was now beaming with delight, whilst Ruby, who had almost fallen over in her rush to get started, was so excited that she had completely forgotten about Amelie currently using her spare bedroom.

As Amelie's story grew into a fascinating article, she relaxed into her normal working mode and allowed her thoughts of the weekend to retreat to the corners of her mind. Confident in her writing abilities, Amelie was still a little concerned whether this particular article, would impress both Stan and Bob enough, that they would send it to print for inclusion in one of that week's editions. It was quite extraordinary that the brief time Amelie had spent with Henry and Clara, had given her such a depth of feeling about them, both as a private couple and from their business perspective. Amelie was flying with creativity in her writing and those watching her, were in awe of the speed at which she created her work.

Already highly respected on the reporting floor, Amelie was about to further impress her male colleagues, with the piece about the great Henry Ford. Stan and Bob sat down to read it. As Amelie watched from a distance, she felt slightly nervous, but before long congratulations were being given by both Stan and Bob, for such a well-written article. Amelie was absolutely thrilled and so over-joyed that she almost skipped along on her way home.

Having already decided to make a pot-roast, once everything was prepared and in the oven baking, Amelie busied herself in the kitchen before glancing at the clock, thinking that Ruby was a bit later than normal and hoping she hadn't lost sight of the time. It wasn't long however, before Ruby's key turned in the door, her excited voice calling out hello and apologising for being late. Not that either was the other's keeper, but they had developed a considerate appreciation of each other, in the time they had shared the apartment.

"Here, I have a nice treat for us, it's a lovely dessert that Ms Madison's cook gave to me, she had made too much anyway and because I was so late leaving, she let me have enough for the two of us." Ruby smiled at Amelie as she uncovered the basket to show her their treat, then continued excitedly, "I have some amazing news Amelie, although, on the way home, I realised that you may not think it such good news, but anyway, let me tell you all about today." Ruby was so excited and quickly began relaying the day's events, including Ms Madison's decision to move and her fabulous offer of taking Ruby with her. Realisation dawned on Amelie quicker than it had on Ruby, as her friend's tale unfolded. But, not wanting to outstay any welcome, or to make Ruby feel guilty in any way, Amelie insisted she did not worry and that when the time came, Amelie would find another apartment.

"Well, that's the other great part about it all Amelie, there's no need for you to move out just yet. Ms Madison has suggested you stay in the apartment and look after it, then, when she next wants to use it, you just make arrangements to stay in a guest house or something. Anyway, Ms Madison said not to worry too much, because once we make the move, which will hopefully be before Christmas, she wouldn't be expecting to come back to New York until at least the Spring! Which is almost a whole year away anyway, so you'll be fine to stay here until then."

Ruby was bubbling with excited anticipation and realising that this meant Bryn could start courting Ruby properly, Amelie couldn't be happier for her dearest friend. It was such a wonderful opportunity and whilst Amelie absolutely understood that fact, she also knew that life in New York without Ruby, would not be quite as shiny and bright as it had been up to now. But, not one to put a dampener on things, Amelie hugged Ruby, as the two of them celebrated the wonderful news. Ruby was keen to send word to Bryn and her family, and so, Amelie ushered her out of the kitchen, saying she was already cooking, sending her friend off to write those very exciting letters.

As Amelie cleared the table and set a place for each of them, she remembered the family meals she had shared in the Carter household, and a small part of her wished she could go with Ruby. This thought was a surprising one, bearing in mind Amelie's enthusiasm at working for the New York Times, but now that she had earned the respect of her fellow workers, her burning desire to be the best, had already been achieved. Today had proved that, when Stan and Bob had raved about her article and congratulated her, stating they would run it the day after tomorrow! Amelie had kept her promise and telephoned Henry Ford from the office immediately, to give him the good news. Which he in turn was delighted to hear and he promised to give Amelie his and Clara's opinions, once they had read the article.

A couple of hours later, with Ruby's letters written and whilst they were sitting eating a delicious meal, Ruby finally remembered to ask Amelie how she had got on with her day.

Chapter 11

An Unexpected Change

Life had been like a whirlwind since their return to New York. Most especially for Ruby, as plans for the move back to Detroit flowed along beautifully. Ruby's letters to Bryn and her family had brought them such joy, that each one of them was buzzing with excitement and happiness. It was a wonderful time for them all. All except Amelie of course. Whilst she was so very happy for her friend, Amelie knew that her daily life would be a lot sadder without Ruby's shining light being a part of it. To distract her from the inevitable loneliness that she expected to feel, Amelie threw herself into her work, making it her main focus and wanting to blot out the sadness, that she knew was going to hit her very soon.

The months were flying by and with several visits to Detroit having been made, to look at houses, Ruby had already been absent for much of the past few months, having to accompany Ms Madison for each trip. Of course, for Ruby, those trips back to Detroit were fabulous, because she had been able to see Bryn and her much-loved family. Amelie had felt quietly envious.

Following each trip back home, Ruby always returned with cakes and gifts from the family, to share with Amelie and often, a lovely letter from Edie and a pressed flower from Frank. The first of which, came as a complete surprise to Amelie, before becoming a treasure she looked forward to following every one of Ruby's visits. Edie's most exciting news had been about the new telephone line that was being installed that week. Edie had written to say how lovely it would be for them to be able to speak on the telephone occasionally, as well as exchanging letters. Amelie had agreed and thought how wonderful it would be to also speak to Frank now and again, too. Edie had secretly hoped the telephone would help Frank and Amelie feel closer, she knew her eldest son had been well and truly bitten by the love-bug, as had Amelie for him.

Frank had made more of an impression on Amelie than even she had previously realised and it was not long before she felt a hankering to see his wonderful blue eyes again and to just talk to him. Amelie was pleasantly surprised by the feelings growing inside of her. It was such a simple gesture for Frank to send her pressed flowers, but because he had made the effort of choosing one, picking it and pressing it, Amelie felt sure his feelings were at least as strong as hers.

With Marjorie Madison's unexpected pregnancy becoming ever more noticeable and feeling keen to escape the disapproving social circle of New York, she had advised Ruby that the big move was to take place soon, in fact, she announced, they would be in Detroit by Thanksgiving. Wanting her baby to be born back home, Marjorie Madison had already planned a quiet celebration, with special friends, who were less critical of her situation. Being so obviously 'with-child' in New York, had been both a blessing and a curse, such was the result of the staunch disapproval Marjorie Madison had experienced from certain members of her social circle.

With Thanksgiving being such a special occasion in the Carter household, the planned celebrations were extended to Amelie by Edie, who had invited her to join the family once again. It was a very welcome invitation which Amelie eagerly accepted, such was her keenness to see all of Ruby's family again, but most especially, Frank. Edie wrote to explain that an invitation to Henry and Clara's home was also included. It seemed they wanted to thank her personally for the fabulous article she had written, which had both delighted and impressed Henry and Clara. Edie had also been asked to tell Amelie, that Henry and Clara had very much enjoyed her company on the previous visit and because Henry wanted to investigate the possibility of another reporting proposal with her, they hoped she would accept their extended invitation. Amelie felt flattered and very excited, she really could not wait to see everyone again.

As the final weeks passed by and the time for the move drew closer, Amelie and Ruby decided a celebration was needed, so, they invited Alfie and Mollie to join them for dinner again. Baby William was growing fast and although his Nanny had now been engaged, the friends had pleaded with Mollie to bring William too. Knowing that William would be cuddled all night, Mollie had laughingly agreed and said she would give Nanny the night off, as she graciously accepted their kind invitation. Having known of the plans for Ruby's move back to Detroit, Alfie and Mollie were also feeling a little sad and thought it a wonderful opportunity for them all to get together again, one last time before Ruby left town.

The evening went so well that before any of them knew it, the clock had struck midnight, bringing their evening to an abrupt end. After several cuddles with both Ruby and Amelie, William had fallen asleep and because he was such a good sleeper, they had almost forgotten he was there during all the laughter and celebrating.

As Alfie and Mollie wished their friends Happy Thanksgiving, they offered good luck wishes and goodbye hugs to Ruby, and a return dinner invitation to Amelie, for when she returned from Detroit, suggesting it would be something nice to look forward to. Amelie accepted with grateful thanks, knowing she would be in need of her friends, when she returned without Ruby. It had been a wonderful evening and as they cleared up the dinner plates, having said their goodbyes to Mollie and Alfie, the two friends shared an impromptu hug, also remarking on how it had been a perfect and happy, final evening together in their apartment. As the last of the dishes were put away into the kitchen cupboard, the two of them bade each other goodnight, before disappearing into their respective bedrooms. Sleep came quickly to them both, despite their earlier excitement and thoughts of Detroit began to invade their dreams in the most pleasant of ways.

Amelie had been grateful to Stan and Bob for allowing her the time off to visit Ruby's family for Thanksgiving and with her train ticket now booked, she shared her excitement about the trip with Bob's Secretary, Julianne, who loved Amelie and was always keen to listen to her plans. Feeling thrilled to be travelling with Ruby on this special journey back to Detroit, Amelie admitted to Julianne that despite being happy to see everyone again, the trip would also be tinged with sadness. Amelie knew it would be a long time before she would see her dearest friend again because this time, Ruby would not be returning with her. In fact, the two of them expected it be Spring-time, before Ms Madison and Ruby returned to New York again. Wishing Amelie, 'Happy Thanksgiving' and very good luck for her next meeting with Frank, Julianne shooed her out the door early, saying Bob had given her permission to do so. Amelie felt very grateful, although slightly unnerved at leaving the office so early. It was not something she ever normally did, but Julianne reminded her of all the extra hours she had already put in and so, accepting the offer, Amelie had almost skipped out the door.

As the three women all boarded the train, Marjorie Madison invited Amelie to join her and Ruby in their private compartment, which was located within the First-Class carriage. It was a very welcome invitation, because Amelie greatly enjoyed the company of Marjorie Madison and they always had wonderful conversations, each having very direct opinions to share and debate over.

During the many months since their shared Titanic ordeal, Ms Madison, who had grown ever closer to Ruby, had often invited Amelie to join them both for dinner. It was during these occasions that the three women, being very modern in their outlook, had shared many conversations about women's rights – both in the workplace and society – with votes for women always heading the list as a priority subject. Amelie felt sure this trip would be just as enjoyable, as far as their conversations were concerned.

The first part of their journey was indeed very pleasant and as the scenery changed, so Amelie experienced a sense of calmness come over her. It was almost as if Ruby's home was now her home and she was on her way to see the people she knew well, and had come to love immensely. As her thoughts strayed to her true home back in England, Amelie wondered how Dylan was doing, her latest letter to him had left two weeks ago and as yet, she had heard nothing from him. But, knowing how busy he would be on the farm, she supposed he would write back closer to Christmas.

Returning to her own carriage, Amelie settled down for the night, knowing that in less than 15 hours, they would be enjoying hugs and family banter. Of course, Ruby would be going off to Ms Madison's new home to begin with, so they would be met by her new driver. Which also meant that Frank would be collecting Amelie from the station – a moment she was very much looking forward to – and then Ruby would join them for Thanksgiving, two days later.

As the rocking motion of the train soothed its passengers to sleep, fifteen miles down the track, two signalmen were struggling to free a jammed junction point. With no other way of warning the fast approaching train, they hurriedly set up noise detonators on the track and positioned red flags, dearly hoping that in the darkness, their warnings would be noticed by the driver. The four o'clock milk train was due to cross the junction just ahead of the train carrying Amelie, Ruby, Ms Madison and their fellow passengers – any moment now in fact – but the points were rigid and just would not move. Because of the darkness, the two signalmen could not see what was causing the problem and both were panicking, knowing a head-on collision would be catastrophic.

Panting and sweating, the signalmen oiled the points and heaved again, suddenly, the tracks moved and they both let out an enormous sigh of relief. The milk-train was on time, but someone up the line had forgotten to tell the signalmen that it had been extended by four carriages and so it was longer than expected. As Amelie and Ruby's train steamed along the tracks, the two men realised the milk train would not clear the junction in time and even as the detonators exploded and the passenger train-driver instantly hauled on the brakes, the passenger train could not stop in time and the front of the engine caught the rear-end carriage of the milk train, causing the passenger train to jump the rails and plough into the fields running alongside it. The two signalmen were already running off to the left at this point, not knowing which direction the train would take as it left the tracks, but ridiculously hoping they could out-run it. With its heavy wheels grinding into the soft earth, the train's carriages began to concertina, unceremoniously shaking everyone out of their beds. People began screaming with fear, as the train lurched and shook everything to the floor. A deafening sound of crunching metal could be heard as each carriage hit the next, the sound ringing out through the stillness of the night. When the shocked driver finally realised he had no control left, both he and the stoking engineer leapt from the still moving engine; unable to do anything more, but not wanting to die covered in burning coals and each knowing they would be needed to help rescue passengers, when the train finally ground to a halt. But the speed of the train was such, that it was not an easy jump and both injured their legs as they hit the ground with a sickening thud. Inside the train, luggage and people were being thrown around haphazardly, unable to hold onto anything long enough to steady themselves.

The milk-train had only lost the rear carriage, meaning the driver had managed to stop safely and as he, and his stoker now ran alongside the tracks towards the passenger train wreck, they both prayed nobody had been killed. One of the signalmen set-off to get help, as the other began climbing onto the now over-turned front carriages to help rescue the distressed and injured passengers. The passenger train's driver and stoker, despite injuries to their legs, also managed to scrabble back to the train and help in the rescue. People were screaming and crying, whilst others were in complete shock and scarily silent, not knowing what had happened, many were stunned, not realising they had blood running from heads, arms and legs. More than a dozen people were trapped, many unable to move at all. The first-class carriages had suffered the most damage, having been concertinaed between the coal truck and the first of the second-class carriages, all of which were now lying on their side. Ruby and Ms Madison's compartment which was closest to the second-class carriage, had been crushed quite severely, trapping the two of them beneath a pile of luggage and twisted metal. Both were unconscious, which was a blessing, in that they were unaware of the terror of entrapment that many other passengers were now suffering.

As men's voices called out to survivors, Amelie, who was conscious, found herself unable to move, her left leg was badly injured and she couldn't scrabble up to the windows, which were broken and just out of reach of her fingertips. Calling out for help, Amelie's voice disappeared into the noise of the screams from other passengers. Worried for Ruby and Ms Madison, Amelie called their names, but it was hopeless. Confused and bleeding from a gash on her head, Amelie fainted with the pain.

When she eventually came-to again, Amelie tried to rally herself, knowing she couldn't rely on anyone being able to help her. Taking a deep breath, she pulled herself up again. As she was about to scream for help, a face appeared at the broken window above her head.

"You alright in there miss?"

The gravelly voice of the stoker from the milk-train, reached her ears through the dusty darkness and she called up to him, telling him she was alone, but she was hurt and needed help to climb out. As he reached down, Amelie grabbed his arm and climbing over the twisted metal, seat-cushions and broken suitcases, she managed to hold on well enough for him to half-help and half-drag her up, and out of the carriage. Reaching the cool night air, Amelie shivered and gratefully thanked the stoker for helping her out.

"We're not quite out of danger yet miss, but you're welcome, now come-on, let's see if we can get you down without injuring you even more."

As more hands reached up to help Amelie, she was thankful of the uninjured passengers, who were rescuing everyone that they could reach. It was a moment of heroism and many men were helping to pull passengers from the wreckage. Whilst the women who were uninjured were trying to help those who were injured. Without medical training, there was little anyone could truly do, other than comfort the wounded by holding their hands and soothing worried cries.

The rescue continued into the night and as blankets, and loose clothing were fetched from the rear carriages, the fire in the engine burned itself out. That was one blessing, had the engine caught fire completely, all of them would likely have been killed in the explosion.

The night was very cool and with only moonlight, there was little to help the rescuers, but they persevered and continued searching carriages.

Amelie had told the stoker about her friends and pleaded with him to search the first-class carriage, but it was impossible. The rescuers could see nothing and the carriage was too crushed to enable anyone to get inside easily.

Meanwhile, from inside those crushed carriages, Ruby was slowly regaining consciousness, but feeling very weak from her injuries. As she tried to call out to Marjorie Madison, Ruby's barely audible voice was unable to breach the outside noise and unsurprisingly, there was no reply from her mistress. Ruby could not see anything, everything around her was black and all she could hear were voices calling out, and people crying. Thankfully, the screaming had stopped, but the cries for help were loud and fear resonated through her. Feeling very scared, Ruby struggled to hear anything more above the grating of metal against metal; her head hurt and she couldn't feel her legs, suddenly, everything sounded muffled and just as soon as she came-to, Ruby immediately fell unconscious again.

Ms Madison was severely injured, her hip having been penetrated by a sharp piece of metal that had severed a major artery, which was now oozing blood faster than anyone would be able to stop. As she lay unconscious, Marjorie Madison's life slowly ebbed away. It was a tragic irony that having survived the Titanic, Marjorie Madison and her cherished unborn child, would end their days here, on a journey back home, inside a twisted train-wreck.

Thankfully, there was no pain and as their souls left her body, Marjorie Madison glanced down at the wreckage, hoping that both Amelie and young Ruby would be saved, before moving into the loving light that was beckoning to her and her unborn child.

Marjorie Madison was just thirty-six years old when she left this world.

As dawn broke, the exhausted rescuers continued searching and were joined by officials and teams of rescuers from the nearest towns. Men came with tools and cutting equipment, whilst doctors and several nurses, who had also joined the rescue effort, were already patching up the wounded, deciding which ones to send to hospital first.

So far, they had established that forty-nine people had been injured, seven of which were suffering from potentially life-changing injuries, and twenty-two also requiring hospital treatment, leaving twenty walking wounded. On the last count, six people had lost their lives, but several passengers were still trapped inside the mangled first-class carriages, one of which was Ruby. The death count was expected to rise as the men managed to cut their way into the crushed compartments.

Amelie watched in horror, knowing there was a strong chance that Ruby and Ms Madison would not make it out alive. When the shock from that realisation hit her, Amelie began to cry and as the tears rolled down her face, not knowing if anyone was even listening, Amelie prayed, begging that her friends be spared.

Two hours later, Ruby was lifted out of the carriage, but it was obvious to the rescuers, that her injuries were severe. Still, they hoped that she could be saved, as they called for a doctor to help.

Someone shouted, "There's another woman in here! Oh, my…" He paused, shocked at what he saw, before shouting again, "She's with-child!"

"Is she alive?"

Leaning into the broken carriage, he strained to see if there was any possibility that Marjorie Madison was breathing "No, she's gone. They both are. There's too much blood, she could never have survived." Tears ran down his face as the man climbed back down.

It was a harrowing rescue for men not used to such things and one which would torment their dreams for years to come. But still they worked on, exhausted, yet knowing they needed to ensure everyone had been accounted for.

As Ruby was being lifted down, Amelie had spotted her hair and realising the limp and bleeding form was her friend, she stood up to go to her, but, unable to walk on her damaged leg unaided, Amelie had to beg someone to help her get across to Ruby. Two kindly women came forward to help her and managed to get Amelie across to where Ruby had been laid on the ground. Leaving Amelie with Ruby, they went off to help wherever they could. Amelie was shocked at how pale Ruby's face was and pleaded to know if she would be okay. The doctor who was working on her friend, quickly realised that it was hopeless and even as Amelie was helped to the ground, to hold Ruby's hand, the doctor looked into Amelie's eyes and spoke the words that would haunt her forever.

"I am so sorry, there's really nothing more we can do for her."

Ruby's eyes opened and she whispered Amelie's name. Squeezing Ruby's hand tightly and trying her best not to cry any harder, Amelie voice was calm and gentle.

"Ruby, my darling, I am here. It's okay, you are safe now my darling, there is no need to worry." Amelie tried to reassure her dearest friend, knowing she was dying and feeling utterly helpless at being unable to do anything to help her, other than reassure her as much as she could, not wanting Ruby to feel afraid.

"It's okay my darling, you are loved so much, you do know that don't you?" Utterly devastated, Amelie knew that all she could do now, was to stay with her friend and remind her of the great love everyone had for her. As Amelie comforted her friend, she could feel a loving warmth surround them and as Ruby weakened, her voice dropped to a whisper and she asked Amelie to tell her family that she loved them, and to say sorry to Bryn that she could not stay... Ruby thanked Amelie for being her best friend... then, as those final words passed across her lips, Ruby's precious soul left her battered body to return home. Amelie broke down and crying with despair, she pulled Ruby into her arms, crying out "Nooooo!"

The two women who had helped Amelie across to Ruby, both returned to comfort her; tears filling their own eyes as they had witnessed Ruby's passing, but no amount of condolence could take away the pain that tore through Amelie's body. First her parents, then Caden and now Ruby, Amelie couldn't bear the searing sense of loss and grief as she cradled Ruby in her arms. The blood on Amelie's face had previously dried and although someone had fashioned a bandage around her head wound, the shock of losing Ruby caused the injury to start bleeding again, quite profusely. The two women tried to persuade Amelie to leave Ruby, so that someone could look at her wound, but Amelie would not let Ruby go and just shook her head. Feeling numb with grief and unaware of quite how badly she was bleeding, Amelie could only be persuaded when she saw her own blood dripping onto Ruby's skin.

"Come on now, my love, you can do no more for her, but you need to have your own injuries checked, you're losing too much blood." One of the women, a kindly, slightly older lady, spoke to Amelie as if she were her daughter and somehow, managed to persuade Amelie to let Ruby go, just as a nurse reached them to re-dress her wound.

The next hours went by in a daze and Amelie, anxious to ensure that both Ruby and Marjorie were identified, would not leave the site of the train-wreck until assurances were made that their names were properly recorded and she understood where their bodies would be taken. Amelie knew she had to be the one to call Ruby's parents, to break the devastating news that would cause a deep and enduring grief, one that would stay with the family forever. It was the last possible thing Amelie could do for Ruby, other than to wait with her, until her family arrived to collect their daughter's body and take Ruby home to their family plot.

That phone call was the hardest thing Amelie had ever had to do, since losing Caden. Crying and shaking with her own pain and grief, Amelie was thankful that Mike answered the telephone. On hearing the distressed voice of Amelie, he was immediately concerned and listened intently, as she relayed the news that no parent wants to hear. Edie, seeing Mike's face crumple, immediately rushed to his side, not knowing what had been said, but aware that something bad had obviously happened. Amelie could hear Mike's despair and then Edie's scared voice, asking what was wrong. As Mike clung to his wife, he told her their daughter was gone, killed in a train-wreck that Amelie had survived. Edie's wailing cry brought the boys running into the house; they too, crumpled in disbelief and grief on hearing their beloved Ruby was gone. The family would never be the same again. But, despite their obvious pain, in that very moment, the strength of their family love rallied them, supporting each other, as they hugged one another and cried, each knowing they wanted to bring Ruby home as quickly as possible. At the other end of the line, Amelie was silent, her obvious shock at being the only one to survive, made her feel culpable and she wished she could tell them that Ruby had survived and that it was all a mistake. As Amelie quietly repeated the last words that Ruby had asked her to pass on to her family, Mike and Edie buckled; Ruby loved them all dearly and was thinking of them as she lost her own life.

As Mike tried to make sense of what Amelie had told him, he knew he had to bring Ruby home and called Henry and Clara to break the news about his beloved girl, and their own dear friend, Marjorie Madison. With no close living relatives, Henry and Clara said they would take care of Marjorie, and Henry suggested to Mike that they travel together to bring both women back home.

It was a journey that neither man would ever want to have to make and for the most part of it, they travelled in silence, united in grief, whilst trying to stay strong for each other. Two sets of glassy-eyes watched the road ahead as the miles swept by.

Clara stayed with Edie and the boys whilst their men were away, wanting to comfort her oldest friend, yet knowing that nothing could take away the pain of them all losing their beloved Ruby.

Chapter 12

Bringing Ruby Home

Exhausted from her ordeal, Amelie waited at the hospital until Mike and Henry arrived to collect Ruby, and Marjorie Madison. With nowhere else to go, having been treated for her own injuries and advised not to walk on her leg for the next few weeks, Amelie realised she would need help. Crutches had been issued to her, along with the strict instruction to rest and allow her crush injuries a decent amount of time to heal. The doctors were surprised there was not an obvious break, adding that only time would tell how well her leg would recover and that physical therapy would likely be necessary, along with much patience, as she progressed through a slow healing process.

By the time Mike and Henry arrived, it was too late to travel back the same day, so they checked into a nearby boarding-house before heading to the hospital to find Amelie. Visiting times had been extended for those relatives who were arriving to arrange transportation of their deceased loved ones, back to their home towns. Extra rooms had been reserved, so that relatives could say their goodbyes privately and it was in one of these rooms that Mike found Amelie. As he walked in through the door, Amelie broke down, unable to hold back her grief any longer. As she fell into Mike's open arms and with tears streaming down both of their faces, clinging together, the two of them stood beside Ruby, who had been laid out, with a white sheet covering all but her face.

As Mike gently let go of Amelie, he leaned down to kiss

his daughter's face, her soft skin, now cold to the touch, was final confirmation to Mike that she really had gone, and that all of this was not just some horrible mistake. Feeling heartbroken, Mike pulled Ruby into his arms and cradled his daughter for one last time, before laying her back down to rest in peace forever.

Amelie immediately began apologising, her guilt at being the one to survive, had been growing throughout the day and was overwhelming her even as she said the words. Although Mike was grief-stricken, there had not been one moment where he had even entertained that thought and told Amelie as much. She was not to feel any guilt and to know that they were all very glad she had survived, and that Ruby had been blessed to have such a good friend with her in her final moments. That fact alone had brought the family great comfort and, Mike added, both he and Edie would be eternally thankful that Amelie was there to hold Ruby's hand and to comfort her as she left this world.

The two stood for the longest time, grieving their loss, telling Ruby how loved she was, and how they would never forget her. When Mike and Amelie finally left Ruby, they walked along to the mortuary reception to make arrangements for Ruby to be taken home. Henry was waiting patiently for them both, having felt it appropriate to leave them to have their final moments alone with Ruby before he too went in to say his goodbyes. Telling Mike not to worry about any expenses, explaining that he and Clara wanted to pick them up, as a small gesture of their love for dear Ruby, Henry proved to be a great support and Mike appreciated their friendship even more.

Once Henry re-joined them, they all headed back to the boarding-house. Amelie, on her crutches, with Mike and Henry walking either side of her, ready to catch her should she stumble. The three of them were conjoined by their immeasurable sense of loss.

Arrangements had been made for the following day and it was agreed they could escort the private ambulance that would transport both Ruby and Marjorie back to their home-town. Once there, both women would be taken to the Funeral Director's Chapel of Rest. Ruby would lie in an open coffin, so that Edie, Bryn and the boys could visit her one last time, before the final funeral arrangements were made.

Marjorie had no living family that any of them knew of, so Henry said that he and Clara would ensure all appropriate notices were posted and arrangements made, subject to any further instructions from her lawyer. Henry hoped the lawyer might identify a relative, because he could not bear to think of Marjorie having just themselves and the Carter family at her funeral.

When Mike and Amelie finally arrived home, Edie rushed out to meet them, falling into Mike's arms, whilst shaking her head in disbelief as tears filled her eyes once again. The two of them held onto each other and cried together. The love and sense of loss they felt as Ruby's parents, could not be measured.

Watching his parents, a red-eyed Frank then stepped forward to help Amelie from the car, as he also thanked Henry and Clara, both for their love and support. Advising that thanks were not necessary because they were like family, Henry and Clara left them all to their private grief, saying that they would call back tomorrow.

As their friends drove off, Mike and Edie stayed outside, each supporting the other as their grief took over. Amelie, who was still feeling rather weak, leant on Frank's offered arm, grateful for his support, whilst Peter held onto her crutches. Very aware of the grief that

Ruby's brothers and Bryn were so obviously feeling, Amelie felt humbled by their joint concern for her, as they all helped her into the house, leaving Edie and Mike to their private grief. The two of them would take a very long time to recover from the sudden loss of their only daughter. If that was even possible.

It was sometime later that evening, after relaying the events as she knew them and having cried with Mike, Edie, Bryn and Ruby's brothers, that again, Amelie took Frank's offered arm to help her to the bedroom. Exhausted from the trauma of the past two days, Amelie was shocked that Ruby's room had been offered to her and as she said as much to Frank, he just replied with, "Ma said it's what Ruby would have wanted."

Feeling honoured and humbled at being allowed to sleep in Ruby's own bed, Amelie cried again as she hugged her friend's childhood teddy, breathing-in her familiar perfume, which still lingered in the fur of the old bear.

The whole family managed to get a little more sleep that night. Each of them feeling completely exhausted by the extreme emotions and grief they had experienced ever since Amelie's telephone-call, breaking the worst possible news. Bryn had slept on the couch, unable to face being alone in his own room back at Mable's Guest House. Not in their wildest dreams, or nightmares, had they ever thought that Ruby would be taken from them in such a cruel way and her loss would be felt forever more.

The following morning, as everyone arose and went down to the kitchen, Edie came into Ruby's room to check on Amelie. Feeling very aware of the fact that Ruby's dearest friend had suffered a terrible experience *and* been badly injured herself, they were lucky that she had even survived. Understandably, Edie was extremely concerned at the prospect of losing Amelie too and she wanted to be sure that Amelie was feeling well enough, to get up and get dressed.

Amelie, was still lying in bed, just staring out of the window, watching the clouds scooting across an unusually blue sky. Her thoughts seemed far away as she spoke, "It's almost as if nothing has happened, isn't it?" Without turning her eyes away from the blue skies, Amelie asked Edie the question and, knowing exactly what Amelie meant, Edie agreed.

"It is strange isn't it. Looking out there, it's just another new day and the sun has risen again. It does feel a little chilly outside, but it really is looking like it will be a beautiful day." Edie's eyes filled with tears as, looking out through the open window at the fluffy clouds which seemed to just hang in the clear blue sky, Edie imagined her little girl sitting up there, watching them both. Tears fell once again.

As Edie sat down beside Amelie, she held her like a mother holds a child and thanked Amelie again for comforting Ruby in her last moments. Amelie's earlier strength failed her and she sobbed again as the two of them clutched each other tightly, crying as they both imagined Ruby sitting on a cloud, way up there, high in the sky, above them all, wanting to be with them, but knowing she could not.

Downstairs, the boys fixed breakfast for them all, aware that their Mother needed time with Amelie. None of them knew how to handle their own emotions, let alone their Mother's and Amelie's and to an extent, they reacted as if they were all on auto-pilot. Bryn made his excuses and left, unable to deal with the emotion the family were feeling and wondering how he would ever recover from losing his beloved Ruby. Thanking Mike for allowing him to stay, Bryn promised he would be at

Ruby's funeral and again thanked them all for welcoming him into their home. Keen for Bryn to understand he would always be welcome, Mike walked him out to the front gate to tell him so.

Returning inside, feeling a sense of loss like no other, Mike sat down at the head of the table, aware of everyone and watching them all carefully, as the boys each brought food and crockery to the table. When the task seemed completed, Mike asked them all to sit down and as they did, he spoke.

"My boys, I want you each to know that I love you all, with every breath in my body and no matter what happens, we are and always will be, a family." Mike sighed heavily as he spoke, "Losing Ruby… (he paused again) … losing our girl, is the hardest thing that we have ever had to deal with as a family and I want you all to know, that I am always here for you. We will never forget her and we should talk about her whenever we feel the need. I know your Mother feels the same and I'm sure she will say so, in her own words, but right now, I want you all to know, that we both love you, very much." With that, Mike picked up his coffee cup and watching his boys' tears rolling down their faces, as they each did the same, together they said, "To Ruby."

The whole family visited Ruby to pay their last respects and to kiss her forehead. Each of her brother's had brought a flower from their garden and placed it inside Ruby's coffin. Edie had brought the teddy that Amelie had held the previous night and Mike, well, Mike just brought his love, and told Ruby that she would forever be in their hearts and minds, and that no matter what, they would never forget her. As he kissed her forehead again, Mike whispered that he had been so proud of her and that she had been the most precious of daughter's that any man could want.

After saying his final goodbye, Mike broke down and sobbed his heart out. Edie clung to him, both of them feeling desperate and unable to heal their broken hearts as they let their little girl go.

Bryn could not face seeing Ruby like that, he wanted to remember the vibrant girl he had fallen in love with and would never forget. The family understood and respected Bryn's decision.

Unable to manage living alone, Amelie stayed with Ruby's family and, at Edie and Mike's insistence, she continued to use Ruby's room. It felt wrong to Amelie that she should be sleeping in Ruby's bed, but she was so very grateful for the fact that her friend's family truly wanted to look after her, knowing that it would be what Ruby would have wanted. Yet it was also an offer of kindness, borne out of their own love for Amelie, which had grown from the first moment they had met her. Ruby loved Amelie and they did too. Loving each of them, Amelie finally knew what it felt like to have a loving family supporting her.

The day of the funeral came and as they all stood around the graveside, each one of them silently wished it had been them, instead of Ruby, that was lying inside the simple coffin being gently lowered into the grave. That very act was so final and the ground so cold, that all of them wished they could keep Ruby close, above the earth, where it was warmer.

* * * * * * *

Those thoughts emanated from them all so strongly, that Ruby's soul felt their love and as she watched them from above, Ruby wished she could reach down and hug them all. Emotions didn't die and neither did the soul. That was clear to Ruby now, because she still felt a deep love for her family and dearest friend. The love was so strong and so complete, that when she questioned her Guardian Angel, who was stood beside her to offer comfort and understanding, it was explained that we are all, always connected to those we love and we can send our own loving thoughts and memories to one another through dreams, and telepathic thoughts. Confirming to Ruby that she could send loving thoughts to her own family, to Bryn and to Amelie, and that they too could send theirs to her, brought a strange comfort. It was explained that each would receive her message and although voices would not necessarily be heard, the feeling would be there and it would be very real.

* * * * * * *

As the funeral service came to an end, Ruby watched her family, Bryn and Amelie hugging each other. Their love for her was so obviously displayed through their sense of grief, that Ruby felt strong pangs of longing and guilt. There was nothing she could do physically to ease their pain, but she could send them each a deeply personal, loving thought, which would reassure them of how much they had meant to her. Ruby's Guardian Angel nodded to her and silently passed on confirmation that they would hear her and feel the love Ruby sent to them, which would indeed, bring them some comfort.

* * * * * * *

As Amelie and the family walked away, leaving their beloved Ruby to rest in peace, they each felt a light fluttering brush past them and a sudden sense of Ruby's presence filled their hearts and minds, making them smile inside. Ruby was not gone, she would always be with them, in their hearts, in their minds and in their very souls. One day, they would each see the other again and the familiar love they all felt, would survive the passage of time, no matter how long that reconnection took.

Chapter 13

Moving On

Ruby's family joined Henry and Clara at the funeral of Marjorie Madison, which took place two weeks later than Ruby's. There had been no trace of any family that they could find, at least, none within the state. Whether there was anybody outside of the state could not be guaranteed, but they were assured that every effort would be made by the lawyers, to ensure Marjorie's will was properly managed and her remaining estate donated to the charity of her choice. That charity turned out to be the children's home in New York that had taken on some of the orphaned children rescued from the Titanic.

Amelie had contacted the newspaper she worked for, the day after the train derailment, informing them of her own injuries and the terrible loss of life for those poor souls who were not as lucky as she had been. Both Stan and Bob had sent their deepest sympathies for the loss of her friends and told Amelie not to worry about her job, that they appreciated it would be a few months before she could return and they promised to hold open her position. Bob immediately decided they would take on a temporary person to help run the stories, for which Amelie was grateful and oddly, she did not feel panicked in any way, even though she expected that her position might have been lost. Knowing Ruby's family were there for her, meant so much more to Amelie and so, she had gladly taken their advice to see-out her recovery with them. They all wanted to help her to get well again.

Ever the reporter, but wanting Ruby and Marjorie to be remembered, subsequently to her first conversation, Amelie had provided enough information for Stan and Bob to run a summarised story, having already cleared it with Edie and Mike, who had given their permission to include a piece about Ruby and Marjorie Madison having survived the sinking of the Titanic, only to be lost in the train derailment. Whilst sympathetic to Amelie's loss, both Stan and Bob were glad of the opportunity to link the Titanic and expand on the story. They were, after all, newspaper men.

Since Amelie arrived at his family's home and whenever possible, Frank made sure he was on hand to assist and keep her company throughout her recovery. It was inevitable that as time moved on, so did their friendship, and both Edie and Mike were pleased to see the closeness growing ever stronger, between their eldest Son and Amelie. Neither could wish for a more perfect choice, should Frank ever pluck up the courage to propose, because they already loved Amelie as if she were their daughter.

The two of them began to spend a lot of time together, talking, reading, laughing as they shared stories from their past. All of which helped Amelie to move on from the pain of the past few weeks. It wasn't just her body that was injured, her mind had been too and yet, the grief they both shared, somehow helped them both to cope with Ruby's loss. Their feelings for each other seemed to grow daily and it was just four months after Amelie had arrived, that whilst helping her to walk down to the stream which ran through a nearby field, Frank decided he would seize the moment to tell her how he felt. Feeling optimistic about how well the two of them got on and knowing the strength of the bond growing between himself and Amelie, Frank had come to realise that he never wanted to be without her in his life.

As the two of them reached the fallen tree that was often used as a seat, Frank helped Amelie to get comfortable and as she did so, he found himself on one knee in front of her. Still holding Amelie's right hand in his, Frank brought her fingers to his lips and pressed a gentle kiss onto them. Amelie blushed, but welcomed the gesture, having also felt her initial fondness for Frank growing into something so much stronger. As Frank looked into Amelie's sparkling green eyes, he gasped at her beauty and reached out to touch the cascade of soft, reddish-brown curls that framed her beautiful face and which she had recently taken to wearing loose. Frank smiled at Amelie and took a deep breath, feeling proud, yet more than a little nervous, his heart felt like it was thumping inside his chest as he gently spoke those well-rehearsed words.

"My beautiful Amelie, since the moment I first saw you, when Ruby brought you home, I have been captivated by you. My dreams have been filled by you and for many weeks and months, I have longed to hold you in my arms and kiss you passionately..."

Feeling slightly nervous and having felt that same urge herself, on more than one occasion, Amelie gasped and momentarily held her breath as Frank continued, feeling a little more nervous with each word he spoke.

"...I know that we have not really courted in the way most folk do these days, but I have found a deep and passionate love growing inside of me and it is because of you, Amelie. I have grown to love you with every inch of my being and I cannot bear to think of you leaving here to return to New York. I know this may feel quite unexpected Amelie, but I desperately want to spend my whole life with you and so I ask you, with every breath I have, baited and waiting for you to say yes... Amelie, will you do me the very great honour of becoming my wife? I promise I will cherish and love you forever..."

Frank's words faded as happy tears sprang into Amelie's eyes and she found herself nodding, "Oh, Frank, I too have found a love growing for you and I have been dreading the thought of leaving you behind..."

As Amelie said those words, Frank's nerves disappeared and he beamed at her. Standing up and helping Amelie to do the same, Frank pulled her towards him and kissing her passionately, all the emotion and feelings he had been suppressing were now transferred, as their lips finally met. Feeling weak with the passion that immediately exploded inside her, Amelie was glad of Frank's strong arms and as their prolonged kiss bonded the two of them forever, Amelie drew back and laughing she spoke the words he had dreamed about.

"Yes, Frank Carter, I would be truly delighted to become your wife."

Kissing him again, Amelie felt her own emotions and love over-flowing with happiness, as her body pressed against his and she felt the strength of Frank's passion for her, rising.

Feeling overjoyed and full of excitement, and happiness, each wanted to share this precious moment with the family. Frank, using a strength which seemed effortless, scooped Amelie up into his arms and carried her back across the field. The whole while, the two were smiling at each other, full of admiration and love for the other. As they reached the front path, Edie happened to glance out of the window at the very same moment and shouting for Mike, she ran outside. Edie's first thought had been that Amelie was hurt, but as she looked at

Frank's face, Edie realised that this was nothing more than good news. Mike followed Edie almost immediately and as he stood beside her on the front porch, he realised his son had achieved a long-held dream. Before Frank had even set Amelie down, excitement gushed out of him as he joyfully reported their wonderful news.

"Ma, Pa, I just asked Amelie to marry me and she said yes!"

As Amelie looked at their surprised, yet happy faces, she just nodded and said, "It's true," as both of her future in-laws, rushed forward with open arms, smiles and happy tears brimming.

Frank set Amelie down just as Edie reached out to hug them both and as Mike joined in and hugged them all, he simultaneously patted Frank on the back. Both he and Edie uttered their congratulations, amid happy laughter and more smiles. What a joyful moment for their family, after all of the sorrow. Mike and Edie felt blessed once again, as they each silently sent out thanks for this wonderful news.

When Frank's brothers returned home, the celebrations really began and the whole family joined in, raising glasses to the happy couple. To Amelie, it was confirmation that she was now and forever would be, part of this loving family and as she silently thanked Ruby for coming into her life and allowing Amelie to join her on that first trip home, after their Titanic ordeal, Amelie knew she belonged here. Thoughts of returning to New York were forgotten, no longer wanted, or needed.

The apartment Amelie and Ruby had shared was being sold as part of Marjorie Madison's estate. Which meant that all of Ruby's and Amelie's belongings would be packed-up and shipped to the Carter household. Their arrival was expected any day now and was one that Edie and Mike, as well as Amelie, anxiously welcomed, whilst knowing the contents would bring both heartache and comfort.

With a wedding to plan, Edie and Amelie had made a pact to keep positive and looking forward, knowing it was what Ruby would have wanted them to do. Also, very aware that they would have good and bad days along the way, but they each hoped that Ruby's bright and chirpy soul would be with them the whole time and boost them whenever they needed it.

* * * * * * *

From somewhere within a spiritual realm, Ruby watched and wished she could be there with them properly, so they could see her, as well as feel her presence through the love she sent to them. It was as though their shared love knew no bounds and Ruby's, now untied from Earth's gravity, could expand ever further, reaching every possible segment of their lives. Knowing that to be true, lifted Ruby's own soul even further.

* * * * * * *

When the happy news of Frank and Amelie's engagement was shared with Henry and Clara Ford, they were overjoyed for the happy couple and Henry immediately offered to speak to the Editor of the Detroit News, to get Amelie onboard as a local reporter, now she was to be staying with the Carter's. Still in recovery, Amelie thanked Henry for his kind offer and said she would indeed be happy to do some real work again, albeit, office based. There would be no hopping around the state for her just yet.

Having already informed Stan and Bob about her new engagement, Amelie had thanked them for their kind understanding, explaining that she would not be returning to New York after all. Both Stan and Bob were disappointed to lose Amelie, her appointment had all but shaken up their previously dull office and her valuable contribution would be a great loss to them, but with the generous and true spirit they felt for Amelie, both men wished her all the luck in the world for her new life, each appreciating how much Amelie deserved their good wishes, after all that she had been through.

Amelie also decided to write to Dylan and tell him her news, knowing he would likely be disappointed to hear she was marrying, but hoping he would understand the reason for her decision to stay in America.

It seemed that there was so much to think about right now, that the days and weeks flew by. Frank was a treasure and his love for her knew no bounds as Amelie basked in his love, knowing that Caden would have approved of her choice. Frank was a very decent man and she loved him a little bit more every day.

Amelie's new life was to be with Frank – who also happened to be doing very well with Ford Engineering – and for the first time in a long time, she felt able to look forward to a bright future as part of a couple. The only remaining piece to their jigsaw of life, was their own home and with their wedding just a few weeks away, Amelie wondered where the two of them would live. After all, as welcome as they were, they couldn't stay with Edie and Mike forever.

The packing boxes arrived from New York, having taken a little longer than expected, but finally, Amelie now had her few belongings with her, which somehow made her feel a little more complete, despite the fact that she still had very little, compared to what she had lost on the Titanic.

The opening of Ruby's boxes had been left to Edie and Mike, and sure enough, there had been many tears, but there had also been smiles, as they found a little diary that Ruby had kept, in which she had shared her love and joyful appreciation of her family home, and the people in it, her parents most especially. To see Ruby's handwriting telling them both how much she loved them, was a great comfort to Edie and Mike. Those precious pages would be read over and over again, throughout their lives, until the paper became worn and tattered around the edges.

Frank found them a small place to rent in town, not too far from the family home, but far enough for Amelie to feel it was *their* home. A place they could decorate and fill together, just for the two of them and without fear of someone bursting into the bathroom, just as they had sunk into a tub after a long day at work. It was perfect and with the help of Edie and Mike, the happy pair soon had it fixed up and ready for them to move into, on their wedding night.

Friends and neighbours had been most generous, giving them lots of bits and pieces of furniture and crockery to get them started. Even Mollie and Alfie had given them a most generous financial gift, to help them start their new married life. It was an unexpected and greatly appreciated surprise, which Amelie was quite shocked by, but Mollie and Alfie had dismissed any concerns and said it was entirely their pleasure to finally see Amelie happy, and they were delighted to have been invited to their marriage celebration.

Henry and Clara wanted to buy them a bed as a wedding gift, saying they had to start on a fresh bed for their marriage. Knowing such a fabulous piece of furniture was a major expense, for which the young couple's money could be better spent elsewhere, Clara and Henry hoped Amelie and Frank would welcome their offer. In truth, the bed was an extremely generous gift which was very much appreciated by Amelie. Frank however, was less bothered about their bed being new, he just wanted Amelie for his wife and in his eyes, any bed would do. That said, he did also appreciate the generosity of such an amazing gift and made sure he thanked his Uncle Henry and Aunt Clara personally.

Despite their recent engagement, the two of them had not yet made love, both wanting to wait until their wedding night and enjoying the anticipated excitement that grew with every passing day. Although that wait was tricky for them both, with several occasions arising where they had been tempted to break their pledge, luckily, something had managed to hold them back each time. That moment was to be special and precious, in their own bed, in their own little house, as husband and wife.

As Amelie and Edie finished preparing the new house for the wedding day, they both stood facing each other and hugged for the longest moment, each wishing Ruby was with them, but grateful for the fact that she had brought Amelie into the family. Frank was working and knowing the two of them would be finishing off the tidying-up and sorting out at the new house, he called-in on his way home from work to find them both hugging. As he joined them, Frank kissed their foreheads and said Ruby would be so proud to see them all together, here, in his and Amelie's lovely little house.

With tears wiped away and the front door now locked behind them, Frank took the key and reminded Amelie the next time she was to set foot-inside, would be after he had carried her over the threshold. Amelie and Edie laughed and cheered up at that very happy thought.

The wedding day arrived and, as hoped, the sunshine woke them all with a happy feeling of anticipation at what would be happening later. One by one, the excited family arose, breakfasted and then Edie saw off the boys, to go and make sure Frank was awake.

As it turned out, Frank, had actually awoken before any of them, as he and the friend he had stayed with overnight, were sat outside, soaking up the morning brightness and looking forward to the day ahead. The boys arrived amid much laughter, with all of their clothes for the wedding, pressed and ready to change into. They had decided to accompany Frank to the church, along with his best-man, which also meant Frank's entourage would be larger than Amelie's.

Amelie was to get dressed at the family home and would be given away by Mike, who had told her he would be prouder than proud, to walk her down the aisle. Edie, feeling very emotional, kept dabbing at the corners of her eyes, as she too felt proud to be involved in this happiest of occasions.

Amelie and Frank were to be married in the early part of the afternoon, so that their guests could all enjoy sitting and dancing outside, as they celebrated the happy event. Edie's friends had all been baking and preparing the delicious food that they would each bring along to the front garden of Mike and Edie's after the ceremony. The men-folk had been tasked with bringing and setting-up the extra tables, cloths and chairs, so that between them, along with the jars of hand-picked flowers on each table, the front lawns would be transformed into a very special wedding venue.

With tears of happiness and joy at Frank and Amelie's union, the Carter family, along with their many friends and neighbours, clapped and cheered when the happy couple took their first kiss as man and wife. Walking back along the aisle and out into the sunshine, the two were beyond happy and as they clasped hands, they kissed again, just as they were showered with home-made confetti and flower petals. Henry had brought along his finest automobile and decorated it with white ribbons stretched across the bonnet. Looking at the beautiful motor-car in the sunshine, as Amelie and Frank ran towards it, they felt even more excited, this fabulous motor was the icing on the cake for their special day, a thing of beauty and because of their love for it, they felt like a King and Queen as Henry's chauffeur drove them from the church, back to the Carter family home. Reaching the house before everyone else, Frank jumped out and ran around the car to help Amelie out, giving the two of them a private moment to tell the other how happy they were and how much they loved each other.

It was the sweetest moment of Frank's life and he knew, in that moment, that he would love this woman for the rest of his days, Amelie was his world and nobody else could ever take her away from him.

The afternoon flew by as everyone enjoyed the happiest of wedding celebrations. Jugs of punch were shared around, along with plates of food and home-made cakes, followed by dancing to music played by a group of local musicians, who entertained everyone with different musical styles and songs. As the night drew-in, the final guests left, amidst cries of congratulations and happy thanks, for a wonderful time.

Amelie and Frank kissed Edie and Mike goodnight, thanking them both for everything they had done.

Edie and Mike glowed with happiness and pride at their eldest son, finally wed and looking forward to a happy future with their beloved Amelie. As the two of them shooed the newlyweds off, they wished them a happy wedding night and said to come back for a family dinner the following Sunday. After many thanks and hugs for both parents and brothers, Frank and Amelie said their goodbyes and made their way to the automobile, so generously left at their disposal for the evening, by Henry and Clara.

When they arrived outside their new home, both Frank and Amelie thanked their driver. As they walked through the gate, Frank gave Amelie the key and then swept her up into his arms. Laughing, the two of them managed to unlock the door and walk through it, without Frank dropping Amelie. Once inside and with the door closed behind them, Frank didn't put Amelie down, instead, he carried his new wife up the stairs to their bedroom, where he gently set her back on her feet, before taking Amelie into his arms and kissing her more passionately than he ever had before. Frank needed her, he wanted Amelie desperately and he could tell she felt the same. As their passions rose, Frank turned Amelie around to unbutton her dress, slipping it from her shoulders. He drew in a breath of astonishment at her naked beauty. Amelie gasped as Frank's lips brushed a kiss on her bare skin. Her own need to feel Frank inside of her was growing with every moment and as he began pulling the pins from her hair, she shivered with anticipation. His hands ran through her rich curls, causing her hair to cascade onto her naked shoulders and kissing her bare skin again, Frank's lips felt soft and sensual. Unable to resist him any longer, Amelie turned around to face him, then slipped her panties off to reveal her completely naked and perfect body. It was Frank's turn to gasp again, as he took in every inch of his beautiful wife, his eyes quickly roaming downwards to her breasts, now heaving in anticipation and on to the mound of soft hair that covered her most private of parts.

"Oh, Amelie, you are so beautiful, I just can't…" Frank's voice faded, his emotions taking over, as his body ached for her.

Amelie took Frank's fingers and after kissing the golden wedding band she had given him a few hours ago, she placed his hand to her naked breast. Frank's touch encouraged her nipples to immediately harden beneath his fingers, he smiled as he gently pulled her towards him, so she could feel his hardness growing for her. Amelie's hands began undressing Frank, unbuttoning his shirt, as he kicked off his shoes, before unbuckling his belt and dropping all of his clothing to the floor, revealing his passion, strong and proud, showing itself in its finest glory… Amelie was left in no doubt as to how much her husband wanted to pleasure her. Frank's heavy sigh was filled with passion, as he lifted Amelie up and she wrapped her legs around him. Feeling Frank's hardness nudging up against her, Amelie begged Frank to lie her on the bed, she wanted him to explore every inch of her with his mouth. He immediately sucked on her nipples and gently stroked her most sensual parts, before slipping his fingers inside her, feeling the warmth of her wetness, just begging for him to pleasure her. Amelie needed to feel Frank inside her as much as he wanted to penetrate her warmth, and yet, they both wanted to tease and play… but their passion had been kept pent-up for far too long and as Frank's lips left her nipples to kiss her again, so Amelie welcomed him to push his hardness inside her. The two of them automatically and rhythmically moved together as one, slowly at first and then ever more urgently, as they worked up towards a shuddering, climactic explosion. Both of them cried out, as their love was consummated and Frank's seed made its way deep inside Amelie's soft belly, to penetrate a tiny cell.

This moment had been worth the wait and as each of them relaxed after the explosive passion of their love-making, they laughed, relieved that neither had let the other down. Far from it, their love-making was perfect and had more than lived-up to both of their expectations.

As they lay in each other's arms, Frank kissed Amelie again, promising to love her forever – words which were music to Amelie's ears, knowing she too felt the same intense love – and as she repeated those words of love for Frank, he again began stroking her skin, feeling his way around her body, holding her beasts in his hands before teasing her nipples. His kisses explored every inch of her and the wanting passion she felt was encouraging her to raise herself towards him, wanting to make him hard again so he could penetrate her once more. Frank desperately wanted Amelie, he wanted to make love to her every night and every morning, and right now, his body was aching for her again. Amelie's fingers gently pushed and pulled, her touch was so erotic, he could not believe his hardness was growing again and she would not stop... not until he could stand it any longer. Moving on top of Frank, Amelie opened her legs wide as she invited him in again and sliding down easily, she smiled as he placed his hands on her hips, holding her firmly as he pumped and pleasured her, until he finally emptied every last drop of his seed into Amelie's welcoming belly.

Exhausted, the two of them fell asleep in each other's arms, the strength of their love for each other was now fully consummated and they slept together for the first time... a husband and his precious wife.

The morning sun woke them early and when Frank

looked across to Amelie, his passion and love for her grew again, he could not control it, just looking at her naked body and beautiful face had him reaching out to touch her. Frank's heart swelled as Amelie smiled back at him.

"Good morning, my husband."

"Good morning, my beautiful wife."

As they lay just looking at each other, their smiles grew, along with their strong desire for each other, until finally, too irresistible to ignore, Amelie reached to stroke Frank's face before she moved to sit astride him again. Frank was in awe of Amelie and he watched her nipples harden as she settled on him again, reaching his arms around Amelie's back to hold her in place, he sat up and with Amelie still astride him, Frank took her nipples into his mouth and sucked, causing Amelie to cry out with a fast-rising passion and wanting for him to have her. Their love-making was more than she could have ever imagined. Frank was so strong and passionate, yet, gentle and loving, his touch was electric, like nothing she had ever felt, as all thoughts and memories of making love with Caden faded into the background. Frank was her man and there was no doubt in her mind that he wanted her, as his lips and fingers pleasured her, before pushing his own hardness up into her again and again. Pulling off of him ever so slightly, Amelie teased Frank a little, smiling wickedly as she rode him until his control was lost and he filled her with a now familiar warmth. As Amelie's own passion reached its peak, her muscles clenched Frank so tightly, he could not believe he was ready to go again, but he did exactly that. This had never happened to Frank before, or to Amelie and the pleasure they both felt was sublime, satisfying them both beyond anything they could imagine. As it would again, every time they made love.

Chapter 14

Family Life

Fulfilling a much-longed for dream, Amelie and Frank's first night of love-making did indeed result in their first child. A fact which caused a lot of teasing and frivolity in the Carter household, as their very exciting news became ever more apparent with each month that passed by. Amelie's tummy grew comfortably and she felt remarkably well throughout her pregnancy. Both she and Frank would regularly caress her tummy and tell their baby how loved it already was and how they couldn't wait to meet them. As Amelie got closer to her due-date, her tummy had expanded much more than she expected and despite reassurances from several local women, who dismissed her concerns, saying they all had different experiences of how much weight they had put on whilst carrying their babies, Amelie thought she was obviously going to be one of the ones who would need to work on losing all the excess weight afterwards.

The day Amelie went into labour, she was sitting in Edie's kitchen, watching her mother-in-law baking a weekend treat for them all. Chatting easily, Amelie found it so comforting to be a part of the Carter family and she loved visiting them each weekend. The women had become firm friends and both were almost as excited as each other, about the baby's anticipated arrival. So, when Amelie suddenly gripped the table and let out a loud, painful groan, Edie knew exactly what was happening and grabbed a towel to throw on the floor as Amelie's waters broke and soaked it through. Calling for Frank and Mike, who were delving into the car engine, making sure all was running as it should, Edie excitedly announced that the baby was on its way. Mike jumped into the car and raced off to fetch the doctor, whilst Frank ran inside the house, only to be told to keep his greasy hands away from Amelie, as another contraction bit into her, causing her to cry-out rather loudly. Mike had warned Frank that whenever Edie had been giving birth, she had always been really irate with him for putting her in such pain, often telling him to get the hell away from her. Mike reassured Frank that they had always laughed it off afterwards, as they'd cradled each child and Edie had told Mike that she loved him, and to ignore her rantings during each birth. So, when Amelie reacted in a similar way, whilst Frank was a little shocked, he realised exactly what his Pa had meant. During the moments between contractions, they tried to get Amelie upstairs to Ruby's bedroom – the family still called it such, even though it had been Amelie's room before she had married Frank – each step-up was a slow process, because the pains were coming surprisingly quickly for a first-born. Part of which, Amelie was grateful for, knowing that the closer the contractions were, meant the sooner the baby was ready to come out, but the other part of her wanted to kill someone as each pain gripped.

It was several hours later when, just as Amelie was beginning to think the baby would never come, out popped a beautiful blonde-haired baby girl. She was totally perfect, a gorgeous little darling and the family oo'ed and ah'ed over her until several minutes later, when another unexpected and massive contraction gripped Amelie. Panicked, Amelie cried out, "What's wrong?"

The doctor, who had arrived in time to deliver Amelie and Frank's baby daughter, lifted the sheet draped across Amelie to check what was happening, just as another baby's head crowned and he delightedly announced, "There's another one!"

Frank looked like he was about to faint. Mike grabbed his arm and held onto him as Edie exclaimed excitedly, "Oh, Amelie, TWINS!"

Amelie looked horrified and threw a look at Frank that scared the bejesus out of him, as she again yelled out and with an almighty push, brought their baby son into the world. As the doctor held him up and spanked his little bottom, the boy let out a comforting cry, joining-in with his sister, who was now lying in Edie's arms.

None of them had expected twins and the doctor had only ever heard one baby's heart-beat, but as he explained later, that does sometimes happen when one baby is hidden behind the other. Amelie delivering twins, came as a massive shock, but as the shock wore off, they were both overjoyed to become the very proud parents of their babies and the fact they had a boy *and* a girl, was like a little miracle to them. Like Edie and Mike had been with their own babies, Frank and Amelie were immediately completely in love with their twins. Nobody could have been prouder in that moment, than Mike and Edie, these babies had brought a refresh of their immense and unconditional love for their family. A family that was now, not-so-little.

Edie and Mike were overwhelmed with love, and when Amelie and Frank announced they were planning to call their baby daughter, Ruby-Jean, both doting grandparents cried with joy. Ruby-Jean, so named, after their beloved Ruby and Amelie's own mother. Whilst Ralph-James was named after Amelie's father.

The utter joy of a new baby in the family was more than they could have possibly imagined, but to now have two little ones to shower with love and affection, well, those babies were sure to be spoilt and loved by every member of the family, as they each came into the room and took turns to cuddle them. Proud uncle's making promises to them that would see both babies into their teenage years.

Life was good for Amelie and Frank, and their work fitted-in well around bringing up their babies. The support they had from the Carter family was incredible, in fact, so much so, that Amelie often remarked to Edie, how they would never have coped without all the help they had received. The boys were always happy to help and Edie had become a very willing and devoted Nanna. Edie hushed away that comment, telling Amelie that of course she would have coped, knowing full well just how very capable her daughter-in-law was. Amelie thanked Edie for her generous kindness and blessed the day that she had become a part of the Carter family.

As the weeks and months went by, Frank's promotion at Ford's meant he was a little more absent than they had been used to. Finding himself working longer hours to help provide for his new family's needs, for the most part, Frank didn't mind too much because it made him feel proud to provide for Amelie and their children. Frank loved his work and was the proudest of new father's as he shared the babies progress with his work-mates, several of whom had become fathers' themselves.

Unlike most workers in her situation, Amelie's boss had very quickly realised she was a winner and didn't want to lose her talents, so had always paid her very well. The extra money that Amelie had been able to bring-in, meant they didn't need to struggle as much as some young families did. But Amelie was now finding the balance between work and family more testing; aside from the lack of decent sleep, she desperately wanted to spend more time with their children, now they were of an age that they were into everything and wanting to learn about the bright new world around them. So, after several considered conversations and looking at how they would manage financially, Frank and Amelie decided she would give up working to become a full-time mother to their children.

Whilst Edie had been a major help to them, the new parents also appreciated that Edie had surely done her time in bringing up children and these two little ones were their responsibility. It became an arrangement that perfectly suited the whole family, leaving Edie to enjoy the odd overnight stay – she just couldn't resist having lots of cuddles and was happy to give Amelie and Frank a break on a regular basis – whilst Amelie adapted easily to the freedom of not working and being able to enjoy her children even more. Frank of course, was just happy to see his little family thriving and would do anything for them.

All was well until an unexpected letter arrived for Amelie. It was from Dylan, explaining that he had joined the forces battling the Great War in Europe, and would already be in France by the time the letter reached her. Knowing Amelie would worry, Dylan explained how he wanted to reassure her, that he would be just fine and would carry her letters with him, to read over and over, to remind him of her and of home. Dylan had intended his words to be of some comfort to Amelie, as her letters would be for him, but of course, feeling worried and desperate for Dylan's safe return, Amelie could not dismiss the worry as easily as Dylan's words suggested.

Knowing how worried Amelie was about Dylan, Frank was a marvellous support and as the months and years rolled on, he would do his best to reassure her whenever he could. As the war raged, so did Amelie's fears, intermittently relieved, whenever a new letter arrived from Dylan. It was a terrible war and many lives had been lost. Dylan was in constant danger, but he always reassured Amelie that it was her letters that gave him hope and the will to live through it.

It was approximately two years later, when the twins were almost three years old and just before the end of the Great War in Europe, that Amelie was in their front garden, having picked up the last of the children's toys from yesterday's play-time, she spotted the mail-man rushing towards her, waving another letter from abroad.

Not recognising the hand-writing this time and feeling worried, as she carefully opened the badly stained envelope, Amelie sat on the swinging seat that hung in the sunniest spot on their front porch. Amelie's hands began to shake and her stomach churned with a sense of dread, as she carefully unfolded the piece of battered note-paper inside it. The handwriting was neater than Dylan's and, Amelie noted, looked more carefully written than Dylan's usual scrawl, but the words she had always feared to hear, now jumped right off the page at her. Dylan had been badly wounded. The letter was from a nurse who had found Amelie's own letters in Dylan's pockets. Realising, that with her not being his next of kin, Amelie would not be informed by the Home Office of Dylan's current situation, a kind-hearted nurse – who had taken a strong liking to the young man in her care – had taken it upon herself to advise Amelie in the gentlest of ways, not that the news was in any way gentle, that Dylan's injuries had utterly overwhelmed him and it was expected he would likely not survive more than a few days. Which, the nurse was also sad to advise, meant that by the time Amelie received her letter, it was highly likely Dylan would have already died from his injuries. The kind-hearted nurse wanted her to know that when Dylan had been asking for Amelie by name, she had reassured him she would be sure to tell his beloved Amelie what had happened to him and that he still loved her very much. Tears immediately streamed down Amelie's face as she cried out, "Nooooo!"

Overwhelmed with shocked disbelief and heartfelt pain, Amelie jumped out of the seat and ran down the porch-steps into the front garden, not knowing what to do and with nobody there to comfort her, looking up into the clear blue skies as her knees crumpled, she cried out, 'Dylan!' And with the hand-written note still clutched in her fingers, Amelie sank to the ground and cried until her aching heart could give no more. Devastated by the loss of another dear friend, an overdue longing for home filled her soul and Amelie decided there and then, that she needed to return to England and her beloved Bude. The losses she had endured since coming to America, had become too much for her to cope with. In the back of her mind, Amelie knew there would be a very real element of danger in getting to England, because of the war in Europe, which seemed to rage-on without respite, and whilst she briefly worried that it would not be safe for her children, in that moment, her need for home was so immensely strong that Amelie decided if Frank and her children died with her, that outcome would also be in fate's hands. Amelie was not thinking rationally and any reasoning was momentarily beyond her as she grieved for Dylan.

When Amelie eventually arose to go back inside, she

knew deep-down that Frank would try to persuade her to stay where they were. Frank would state the simple and true fact, that it would be safer for them all to stay where they were. Amelie was sure he would resist travelling to England and it seemed unlikely that she would be able to persuade him, but she also knew she had to try.

It was a couple of hours later before Amelie felt able to wash her face and tidy herself, then making her way over to Edie and Mike's to collect the children. Frank was working late again that day and Amelie had gratefully accepted Edie's kind offer of leaving the children with her, so that Amelie could catch up on her chores at home. Amelie was thankful that the children were not at home when the letter had been delivered, she would not have been able to cope with them during the last few hours.

The walk seemed to take forever and along with the over-powering emotions and sobs that had racked her body along the way, Amelie felt decidedly weak and quite unwell by the time she reached the Carter family home. Edie was playing with the children in the garden when, seeing Amelie rushing towards them, her face now ashen and looking fit to collapse, Edie called out to Ava, their new home-help. Recognising the unusual and fearful tone of Edie's voice, Ava rushed outside to gather-up the children, whilst Edie went to catch Amelie, who was by now, covering her mouth with her hand, trying to prevent the fresh sobs from spilling out and scaring the children.

"My darling Amelie, whatever is the matter, you look done-in. What has happened my love? Are you hurt?" It was obvious to Edie that something was clearly very wrong, because she had not seen Amelie look like this since they had lost Ruby.

"It's Dylan…" sighing heavily, she could barely speak the words. Amelie's pain was clearly etched on her face, as she reached Edie. Still holding the letter in her hand, Amelie's hands shook as she explained that Dylan had been fatally injured whilst fighting the war in France. Her voice had faded to a whisper and she was barely able to speak, as shaking her head and with tears streaming down her face, Amelie thrust the letter into Edie's hand, then fell into her mother-in-law's embrace.

Of course, Edie and Mike knew about the Great War in Europe, they all did and they knew Amelie's dear friend Dylan had recently been sent across to fight, but this brought the true danger of war right to their doorstep. Poor Dylan. Amelie's dearest friend from back home, was himself now a victim of war. Edie hugged Amelie and holding her tight, let her cry until the tears no longer fell.

A while later and feeling emotionally exhausted, Amelie, grateful for Edie's understanding, apologised for her distress, only to have her apologies hushed. Edie understood her pain and holding her close, reassured Amelie that they were all there for her. Keeping an arm around her daughter-in-law, the two women made their way inside the house. Ava had taken the children upstairs to the nursery, with its two small cots. Ruby's bed having been stored away. Still unaware of what had caused Amelie such pain, Ava dutifully entertained the children, whilst Edie comforted Amelie downstairs, saying that Frank would no doubt be home soon.

Frank had become interested in the aircraft used in the war effort and along with Mike, had often talked to Henry about them developing an airplane engine. All of that talk often refreshed worries for Amelie, thinking that her Frank could be called up at any moment. Now, re-sharing her concerns with Edie, she realised that with America having just joined the war, it was a fear that had also been growing inside of Edie. Both Mike and Edie knew their boys were the prime age to be called-up and it was something they had talked about on many an evening, as they settled into bed. So worried were they, that their nightly prayers now pleaded for the war to be over quickly, so that every man and boy involved, could return to their homes, safe and well.

When Frank arrived home that evening, he found the house in darkness. Guessing that Amelie had gone to fetch the children, he presumed they had just decided to stay on for a bit. It was unlike Amelie to keep the children out late, but, knowing his folks well, Frank supposed they had enticed them all to stay for dinner and so, he made his way over to his parent's home, hopeful of a plate for himself.

Edie had already suggested the children stay the night, due to the late hour, so, by the time Frank arrived, they were already in bed and listening to a bed-time story, being told by Ava, who had very kindly suggested she stay on for a bit longer that evening, to help out. Ava had been told the sad news and her heart had gone out to Amelie, also knowing that Dylan was a dear friend from England and very important to Amelie.

When he arrived at the house, Frank was saddened to hear the devastating news about Dylan and relayed his deepest and most genuine condolences to his darling Amelie, as he hugged her through yet more tears. Thanking his mother for taking care of his family, Frank suggested he take Amelie home, so that she could try and get some decent sleep, before returning to collect the children in the morning. Mike and Edie agreed that was best and hugged them both again, saying to Amelie, there was no rush to collect the children and for her to try and get some much-needed sleep. Mike drove them both back in the car, along with a plate of food for Frank.

Once they were home again and able to speak privately, Amelie told Frank of her longing to go home. As she expected, Frank was shocked at the thought of them all travelling to England. Feeling rightly concerned that it would be far too dangerous for their family to travel. Besides, with Dylan already gone, as sad as that was, Frank reasoned that there was little point in taking such a risk at this turbulent time; and knowing her own parents had already died, many years ago and with no other living family, Amelie knew Frank was right, but the longing did not subside.

Eventually, with Frank's calm and supportive reasoning, Amelie realised it would be totally impractical at this time, but she felt cheered when he promised that they would take the children to visit England, once the war was over. Having agreed with Frank's reasoning, Amelie took herself off to bed, adoring her wonderful husband, who had found a sensible compromise. Feeling thoughtful, Frank mused over his suggestion as he made them both some hot chocolate, before he then followed Amelie upstairs. Knowing their children were safe and had gone to sleep without so much as a murmur, both he and Amelie were grateful to Edie and Mike for their constant love and support. Ava too.

Amelie relaxed into Frank's arms, thanking him for being such a wonderful husband to her and caring father to their children. Frank, who felt evermore protective of his family, assured Amelie that he was proud of her and their children, and loved each one of them more than he could ever explain. As Frank spoke those loving words to her, she reached up to kiss him, her spent emotions rapidly reviving with the love they shared and as Frank responded, the two of them began making love. A new intensity was filling their hearts and as their rising passion reached their most private parts, it was as if they were making love again for the very first time. Moving on top of Frank, Amelie could feel his hardness pressing against her and as she guided him inside, his hands found her breasts, squeezing them as their familiar rhythmic movement, found Amelie's wetness arousing them both, until Frank could wait no more and when Amelie's climax began clenching him, he erupted and rushed their third child into Amelie's womb.

Chapter 15

A New Era

As the weeks and months drifted by, the routine of family life settled down again and Amelie found herself becoming more and more intrigued by the reporting of everything that was going on back home. It was now 1918 and women had just won the right to vote, which was very important news to Amelie, who had always been an extremely independent woman. With their third child growing inside her belly, Amelie felt grateful for the fact that Frank was a very modern thinking man, who supported the right of women to vote.

Based on his own experiences and upbringing, Frank had always felt like the women were the ones really in charge anyway and that men were simply, 'bringing food to the table and chopping wood for the fire'. As far as Frank was concerned, men were there to provide for and protect their families, whilst supporting the matriarch in her nurturing of the children, ensuring all their little ones were brought up properly and with goodness in their hearts. Frank felt like the world had it all wrong and that his views were far more progressive and as modern marriages *should* be.

Along with the rest of the Carter family, they would often find themselves discussing the general politics of the day. Sometimes it led to a heated debate, but more often than not, they all ended up on the same page, for theirs was a truly modern-thinking family.

Amelie found herself hoping for a very different future

for their children, especially for Ruby-Jean and knowing how lucky she was to have Frank. There was no way Amelie wanted their daughter's future to be controlled by a man. Frank always laughed when she said that, knowing their daughter was, even at her tender age, already proving to be a fierce little warrior, as was her brother, Ralph-James. Frank was sure that nobody would be telling Ruby-Jean what to do once she was grown.

Frank and Amelie were wonderful parents, who always encouraged their children to be independent and kind to others, whilst being strong enough to stand up for themselves. So far, their plan was working and Amelie loved the fact that her children got the best of both worlds, having a fun and creative environment at the local school, which perfectly blended with the time they spent with their grand-parents and at home. The two of them were happy little souls and as their development took them from strength to strength, Amelie hoped their third child would be just as happy. Having a new life growing inside of her, had managed to stifle Amelie's longing to return to England. Much to Frank's relief.

Sarah-Louise was born without any concerns and thankfully, was also just the one baby. Their second daughter was delicate and fragile, but just as much loved as her siblings were. The twins doted on their little sister and were always so gentle and loving, that Amelie and Frank could not believe how lucky they were. Their children were thriving and loved spending time with their young cousins. Frank's brothers had also married in recent years and each of them had fathered children. The family gatherings on a Sunday had grown beyond even Edie and Mike's expectations. Edie, was evermore grateful for Ava's help as their family grew. All of the grandchildren regularly came to play and enjoy the home-

172

baking that Edie found herself constantly doing; which was no problem for Edie, she had been born to be a home and family-maker, and she relished every moment of it. Mike, on the other hand, watched them all growing with immense pride and gratitude, happy that their family was doing so well. Life carried on and Amelie and Frank's family time developed a happy routine.

In 1922, Frank was promoted into Ford's new aircraft business and was absolutely thrilled to hear of their latest acquisition, which would involve the building of a new airstrip. Life could not have been more exciting for Frank and the natural progression to aircraft engines, was a welcome option for him.

It did not come as a surprise to Mike when Frank's design skills really came into their own and he watched his eldest son with pride, as he fast became a valued member of the aircraft design team.

As the years rolled on and the 1929 Wall Street Crash happened, Mike was nearing retirement and he knew Edie would be glad to have him home more, so when Henry talked to Mike about the financial situation of the company, Mike decided to start himself on a winding-down programme to retire from the business. Knowing he would be able to spend more time with his fast-growing family, Mike looked forward to his retirement with happy anticipation. The grandchildren were all doing so well and the years seemed to be rolling past so fast, that before they knew it, the twins fifteenth birthday was upon them. Mike and Edie hosted a special birthday party for them and with plenty of family helpers, they all had a wonderful time. As they lay in bed that evening, feeling thankful for their wonderful family and the love they all shared, Edie and Mike felt blessed.

As the 1930s continued to bed-in, times began to get

tougher for everyone. The American economy was already struggling and talk of a recession became a reality. Even the Ford Motor Company was beginning to feel the pinch even more, meaning each of the brothers were worried for their job's. Mike was worried too. He knew alot more than his sons about how worried Henry and Clara were. These harder times were testing them all as a family and one by one, the brothers each spoke of moving out-of-state to look for other work. In truth, none of them really wanted to do that though. All three of them had grown up with engineering in their hearts and minds, so the talk never really came to anything more than a last resort option, should that time ever come.

The worry of the struggling economy took its toll on everyone though, particularly Edie and Mike, who still felt responsible for their children and grandchildren's welfare. As a couple, they had always enjoyed good health, but the worry of the recession impacted them more than anyone realised and health issues came along. In the main, they went again, so, it was a very worrying time for the whole family when Edie caught a bad dose of influenza. Having instructed the whole family to stay away, Edie was determined that the children would not catch this awful bug from her. Somehow and thankfully, Mike didn't catch it, which he supposed, was down to Edie insisting he sleep in one of the boy's old bedrooms whilst she was ill. As it turned out, that proved to be a good suggestion because Edie was also able to sleep as much as she needed to, without being disturbed. Assured that sleep and careful nursing had been her life-saver, it was just two weeks later that a relieved Mike was happy to announce to the family they could all visit once more. Edie was over the worst, she was still quite weak, but no longer contagious and seeing her beloved family would give her the vital boost she needed. The family took turns to visit, making sure one of them was always on hand to help and slowly, but surely, with their love and support, Edie made a full recovery.

Mike felt a real concern for his and Edie's mortality during those two weeks, which actually turned out to be a good thing, because he now fully accepted that his decision to retire was the right one. Edie was relieved, because she had been worried that Mike might regret having to retire and whilst she had wanted him to, she knew he was one for keeping busy. Now, she didn't need to worry so much and instead, quietly reflected on how things can happen in mysterious ways sometimes.

As the depression took a firm grip, cutbacks had to be made on everything, including food, which meant many of their friends and neighbours began to catch a variety of illnesses. Edie was certain it was due to the lack of fresh fruit and vegetables, and convinced Mike that they should start a little local co-operative, where, along with their family and neighbours, they could all grow and swap food from their gardens. Between them, the community pulled together as best they could. But it was not enough, at least, that's what Edie said and blamed herself for, when their darling Ruby-Jean fell sick and was confined to her bed.

Of course, nobody knew if the lack of a good selection of vegetables would have helped Ruby-Jean, because the doctors were baffled as to what was causing her illness and could not diagnose what was wrong. It seemed to be a mystery and caused Ruby-Jean to resist eating very much at all. The whole family became desperately concerned.

Life was very hard during this time and the worry of Ruby-Jean's illness beleaguered them all. The family rallied around as much as they could, constantly trying to entice Ruby-Jean to eat whatever treats they could get their hands on, but there was little that anyone could do. Without a firm diagnosis, all of the treatments the doctors suggested had no effect and Ruby-Jean continued to deteriorate. It was as if she was fading before their very eyes and the whole family were beside themselves with worry.

One morning, as the leaves turned golden and the sun shone brightly in a cloudless blue sky, Amelie went to wake her beloved daughter. Finding her skin cool to the touch and her lips and finger-nails blue, Amelie's mind plunged backwards in time, to when Caden had died and she froze, in utter disbelief at this happening again, as she pleaded for it not to be true. But Amelie could see that all signs of life had drained from her daughter's tiny body and Ruby-Jean's time on this Earth was already over. Their beautiful angel had gone back home. Amelie's blood-curdling cry could be heard by all of her neighbours, who came running immediately, afraid of knowing exactly what they were going to find. Frank was already at work and had to be called back home, as neighbours stepped in to fetch Edie and Mike, and to look after Amelie, who was utterly distraught and totally inconsolable.

The days that followed, crawled by with such pain, that the whole family felt it and a state of depression seemed to take over the whole Carter family, as once again, they buried a child far too soon after the last one.

*   *   *   *   *   *   *

Ruby-Jean watched her parents from above, her heart reaching out to them every single night, as she whispered her messages of love into their sleeping minds. They must each know how much she loved them and how sorry she was to have left them behind. Mama, Papa, I love you so much…

Holding her hand, Ruby reassured Ruby-Jean that they did know how much she loved them and that they would always be able to feel her around them, in their dreams and sometimes whilst awake.

*   *   *   *   *   *   *

As the economic depression further gripped their community and having now lost her Ruby-Jean, Amelie withdrew into herself. The grief was so utterly unbearable, that even holding Ralph-James and Sarah-Louise in her embrace, could not heal the deep wounds Amelie felt. Life had become much too hard and once again, her thoughts longed for the sanctuary of England and her beloved Bude.

Frank threw himself into his work to try and manage his own grief, but Mike and Henry both knew he could not survive on so little time away from home. The hours were too long and financial worries too draining. Both men wanted Frank to spend more time with his family, knowing his pain was so very hard to bear and worrying if he would cope well enough to survive.

It was an unchallenged fact that the Carter family had suffered more than most and just as all seemed lost, Henry spoke to Mike about an idea he had. It was one he knew Mike and Edie would be sad about, but it was one that could be the saving of Frank and Amelie, before grief wiped them both out. Henry had received a request from the RAF in England, who were desperate to employ airplane engine makers, particularly engineers and designers. An offer had been proposed which would be very attractive to anyone wishing to take advantage of a new life in England. As Henry explained his idea to Mike, both men's hearts grew heavy, knowing this could be a saving grace for Frank and Amelie, but at the expense of them likely never being able to see them again.

When he got home, Mike spoke to Edie. As parents, they only wanted happiness for their children, but life was breaking Frank and Amelie, and so, as the joint heads of their family, Mike and Edie agreed they would have to be the strong ones and encourage their eldest son, and much-loved daughter-in-law, to start a new life together in England. Both Mike and Edie knew that Amelie had craved her English home for many years, but whilst they felt it to be the obvious option, they were also heartbroken at the prospect of never seeing them again. It would be a blessed relief in one sense, to know their offspring would be safe and happy, but the devastating wrench that they and the rest of the Carter family would feel, was going to be difficult for them all. It was a choice that neither parent wanted to make, but both agreed would likely be for the best.

Realising that they themselves had a limited life-span now, unselfishly, both Mike and Edie wanted to do whatever was best for their children and grand-children, even if that would cause themselves unbearable pain at letting them all go.

Chapter 16

Life Changes Direction

Several months later, as their ship set sail, Amelie's broken heart began to soar again. It was 1938 and she had been away from home for over twenty years, finally, she was going back to England! Whilst Amelie's spirits soared, Frank's emotions were all over the place. Although he was extremely excited at the thought of a safe and hopeful new future for their family, knowing he would be working for the British Royal Air Force (a fact he had been proud to announce to his parents and brothers), Frank was also overwhelmingly sad at leaving them all behind. Having been persuaded by Mike and Edie, he knew he absolutely had to do what was right for the future for him and his family. The fact that his parents had said that he was not to worry about them, seemed ridiculous to him, of course he would be concerned about them and he was devastated to leave them, but both had said they would always be there for him, no matter what happened. Besides, Edie had added, they could keep in touch by letter. Although, it had to be said, Edie was trying to convince herself as much as Frank that exchanging letters would be enough.

This was the first and only time that Frank had ever been away from his family and despite them all promising to do their best to come and visit in the future, they each knew the likelihood of that ever truly happening, was slim at best. Frank couldn't tell Amelie exactly how he felt, because the burden of losing Ruby-Jean had been all too great for them both and their emotions were just about coping as it was. Frank knew they needed a fresh start and he hoped that in some way, giving Amelie her dream of returning home, would bring them all happiness once again. Never before had he imagined how pain could change a man, but it had definitely changed him, of that there was no doubt and he was fiercely protective of his wife and children, despite the fact they too were now young adults. Frank felt convinced they were making the right decision; he knew Amelie needed to be back in England and to see her beloved Bude again. They had all heard so many different stories about the people Amelie knew there, that it was as if they almost knew them, themselves. Frank looked forward to seeing the places and people that Amelie spoke so fondly of.

Unsurprisingly, as the journey progressed, Amelie found she also had mixed emotions, as did Ralph-James and Sarah-Louise, they were all leaving behind the only family they had ever known, including their much-missed Ruby-Jean. But Edie and Mike had been convinced that this would be a good opportunity for them all and would help them move forwards from the pain of losing Ruby-Jean. They would never forget her, not ever, but Amelie knew in her heart, that they each of them also needed to heal and to continue to live. Ruby-Jean would want them to and the move would be especially good for Frank, enabling him to continue his great work with airplane engines and for them all to flourish in a more stable economy.

The British Royal Air Force would be lucky to have Frank and Amelie reassured him of that fact whenever she felt his enthusiasm dip during their journey. The ship was an exciting adventure for them all and they enjoyed spending time on-deck, watching through binoculars, whenever another ship could be seen in the distance. The passion for their new life was re-charged, as they all enjoyed every possible pleasure of being onboard a magnificent ship. Despite Amelie's last experience onboard such a vessel, she coped with the passage very well, only worrying when a storm was predicted, but then quickly reassured by Frank that whatever happened, they would all stay together, e*ven if that meant they died together.* Although he didn't actually say the last bit, not wanting his reassurances to be marred by the thought of early death.

Amelie took comfort in knowing that this time, she had Frank to protect her and their children. Whatever happened to them as a family, they were her life and her future, and no matter what, they absolutely *would* survive together. Of that she was surprisingly convinced.

*   *   *   *   *   *   *

As Caden watched, he willed Amelie to stay positive and endure the pain of losing Ruby-Jean well enough to look forward to a future with Frank, Ralph-James and Sarah-Louise. Caden had known Ruby-Jean's time would be short, because it had been her chosen path, but he hoped Amelie would not allow such a tragic loss to prevent her from living her life to the full, with Frank.

Also watching over them all and sending her undying love, Ruby-Jean needed her family to be safe and as she gently stroked her mother's face, trying to ease her pain, she whispered, "You are doing the right thing Mama, I love you Mama and I am always with you."

Ruby also smiled down at her dearest friend, happy in the knowledge that Amelie would finally be seeing her home again and sending her love too. Ruby wanted to reassure both Amelie and Frank that she would always be with their darling Ruby-Jean.

*   *   *   *   *   *   *

It had been arranged for the family to be stationed in Oxfordshire to begin with, whilst they all settled into their new life in England. The house they were to be allocated meant they would be based at the recently built Brize Norton Airbase, which Frank was grateful for, because it meant they would all be close by and could mix with the other military families.

Frank was feeling the nerves of his family more than Amelie, who was naturally more excited about returning to England. That said, all of them were a little cautious at the massive change this new life was offering, so to help alleviate those nerves and fears, throughout the journey across the Atlantic, Amelie had enthused them all with more tales of her own childhood and how different life in England was, from where they had lived before.

It was an exciting, but also quite daunting prospect for them and of course, there were times when tears for the family and life they had left behind, would overwhelm each one of them. But, remembering how tough life had been throughout the depression, they rallied each other, wanting to keep everyone upbeat and to stay as optimistic as possible about their new, unknown future.

Frank and Amelie knew they had to make this work, because life in America had changed beyond anything they had known in previous years. Losing Ruby-Jean at such a young age had been too high a price to pay and as worried parents, there was no way they were going to allow Ralph-James or Sarah-Louise to suffer the same fate. Which is ultimately, what had kept the two of them focussed on their need for a very different, happier future for their surviving children to thrive in.

The house they were given was newly-built and they were the first family to occupy it. It was a luxury that was not lost on the family and they all appreciated the warmth and comfort the house offered. The rooms were all a good size and having a swanky new kitchen and bathroom had them all smiling.

As boxes were unpacked and their precious belongings spread around the house, a homely feel settled around them and it was not long before familiar family arguments and laughter could be heard. The kindness of one of their new neighbours, when they brought round a delicious cake to welcome the family, was very much appreciated. Although, Frank was sure their secondary motive was also to find out who these American's were, that had caused such a chatter amongst the other families on base. Sure enough, a few days later their neighbour admitted as much and after laughing about it with them all, it was not long before they had all made new friends and found answers to some of the many question's they each had about life in this new place.

Despite having made new friends, the reality of living on-base was very different to what they were all used to. There were some frustrations and tears to deal with, which were not unexpected but, after many heart-to-heart conversations, they each consistently agreed on the most important thing, which was that they were sticking together, as a family, and growing evermore determined to make the best of their exciting new life. It's an adventure, became a new phrase that Frank and Amelie threw into the mix whenever any sadness crept in. Amelie still craved her beloved Bude, but for now, she realised they had to be satisfied with living where they were.

Gratefully accepting the support of their new friends and other RAF families, they soon began to thrive again.

Finally, Frank felt they could truly look forward to a better future for them all. Both he and Amelie had already begun to talk of what they envisaged that future to be, once Frank was no longer needed by the RAF. Both expected to be living in Bude within a couple of years, having decided they would need to set-up a business, to provide an income to support them all.

Letters were regularly swapped with their family back in America and just as promised, Edie wrote back with news of the whole family. All of the cousins had written to each other too, so there was always a letter arriving for one of them, which eased the burden they felt at leaving everyone behind.

As their daily life took on a new routine, Robert-James and Sarah-Louise became more involved in the lives of their new-found friends and before long, they were known by everyone as RJ and Sarah-Lou, which neither of them minded at all. They were just happy to feel accepted and wanted by their new English friends. Life on base was like a little community and because of that, it had come to remind them of their home back in America. There was a comfortable friendliness on-base, which helped them to settle-in really easily and feel part of this new world they were living in. Robert-James had developed a fast-growing interest in the intelligence work that was often quietly talked about, although the actual details of which, could never be shared of course. Everyone just knew and accepted that 'intelligence' was fast becoming a new field of work.

Frank kept his promise to Henry that the Ford name would be offered as a positive influence at every opportunity and being a man of his word, despite his new allegiances, Frank did not forget his American friends. In fact, Frank found that being close to Henry Ford opened certain doors for both him and Robert-James.

In the midst of a busy morning on the first day of September 1939, their whole world changed again, when the British Prime Minister, Neville Chamberlain, announced to the whole country that Hitler had invaded Poland and that Great Britain, and France, had now declared war on Germany.

Security at the base was already tight, but suddenly, all unnecessary personnel, which included all of the families, were advised to seek alternative accommodation. Safety was a prime concern and of course, the base was about to become a whole lot busier with pilots and engineers. Frank was advised their accommodation would be needed.

It was the moment that would set them off on the next stage of their challenging lives, as Frank and Amelie decided that they should take this opportunity to move their family to the South-West of England because Bude seemed a far safer option than anywhere else they could think of. As they all sat around the kitchen table that evening, Frank advised them of the planned move and that he would of course, be returning to the base, but that he would be able to worry less about their safety, once they were settled in Bude. Amelie was worried about Frank, yet excited at the same time, to finally be going home. RJ and Sarah-Lou complained about leaving their new friends behind, but also recognised, that every family on-base was in the same situation and had to be re-located elsewhere. Frank eased their concerns, having convinced them that he could relax more, knowing his family would be safe.

So, once again, with bags and boxes packed, the family

moved to another new home. For Amelie it was like a home-coming and she was overjoyed to see her old friends and neighbours, many of whom had been convinced she was lost on Titanic, until Dylan had received her first letter. Amelie had loved introducing her husband and children to everyone and they had been overjoyed at seeing Amelie happy again. They had all known of the losses that she had suffered when her parents had drowned and Caden had died from his head-injury. So, to see her happy again and settled with a new family, was a true blessing to them all. Of course, many of the people Amelie knew, were now parents and grand-parents themselves, so there were lots of new faces to meet.

Frank was impressed by the number of people that remembered Amelie and as they welcomed him and their children into the Bude community, he was reminded of his own family back in America and despite a brief sadness, he felt relieved that Amelie, RJ and Sarah-Lou would not be isolated. The people of Bude seemed to want them there and were happy to help them in any way they could. Frank said as much to Amelie, which made her beam with relief and delight.

With RJ and Sarah-Lou starting the unpacking, Frank and Amelie left them to it and headed off to the beach, for some quiet time to themselves. RJ and Sarah-Lou totally understood their need for some privacy and generously encouraged them to go and be together, whilst they took charge of the unpacking.

It was a very warm September afternoon and the tide was still out as they strolled along Summerleaze Beach, towards Crooklets and then on to NorthCott Mouth Beach. It was a perfect day, the sun was shining and the water was warm, although Amelie would only paddle in the rock-pools, her fear of paddling or swimming in the sea, having never left her. Frank could see why Amelie had loved this place so much. The beaches seemed almost comforting to them and the people so welcoming and friendly, that he knew they would be happy here and deep inside, Frank knew he wanted to re-join them as soon as he possibly could. This was their new life and he couldn't wait to get back and be together again.

As Frank and Amelie strolled back towards home, he stopped her for a moment and taking her in his arms, he told Amelie that she was the most important person in his world and that he could not wait to return and then he kissed her with a passion that took her breath away. As a warm breeze brushed over them both, enveloping them in a moment of pure love and joy at being together, the two were now one and their love in this place had exploded beyond anything they could have imagined. Frank swung Amelie around and laughing he shouted out, "I love you, Amelie Carter!"

With orders to return to base the moment Frank had settled his family into their new house and despite only having a few days of authorised leave, he managed to see enough of Bude to truly understand why Amelie had loved and missed it so much. The coastline was absolutely spectacular and Frank now felt far happier, knowing his family would be safe there, but also knowing he absolutely wanted to be there too. There was no longer a hankering to return home to America, because this was his new home... *their* family home, his and Amelie's.

When the time came for him to return to *RAF Brize Norton*, Frank kissed his family goodbye, telling each one of them that he loved them very much and would return as soon as he was able. As his train left town, tears streamed down Frank's face, knowing that he had absolutely no idea of when he would get to see them all again.

$$* \quad * \quad * \quad * \quad * \quad * \quad *$$

Watching all of this from above and not knowing the planned outcome for the whole family, Ruby-Jean again sent them thoughts of love as she whispered into her parents' minds... Mama, Papa, I love you... and Papa, be sure to stay safe and return back home to them...

$$* \quad * \quad * \quad * \quad * \quad * \quad *$$

Caden had watched over Amelie as she and Frank had shared their special moment on the beach and he was happy for them both, also knowing that his beloved Amelie was back home where she truly belonged. Ever since Caden had saved Alfie to help Amelie, Caden had watched Amelie's life carefully and whilst he had been unable to prevent every tragedy, he had been comforted in knowing that Frank truly was the best of men. A man who would always do his best to look after his own family and the woman they both loved, Amelie.

$$* \quad * \quad * \quad * \quad * \quad * \quad *$$

Chapter 17

The Journey's End

Despite those well-meant promises and because of the war effort, it was to be another two years before Frank would return to Bude and that visit was only very brief.

Life had progressed for Amelie, RJ and Sarah-Lou as they settled into their new life in Bude, mixing with family friends old and new. RJ had found his interest in intelligence work and the experience of being at Brize Norton was to become of great use. Unbeknown to the masses, there was much intelligence work being carried out in secret, around Bude and RJ had become part of it. Nobody knew, of course, outside of those whom he worked for and RJ felt proud to be trusted; he felt he was following in Frank's footsteps, supporting the brave men who were fighting for the freedom of people.

Sarah-Lou's interests lie-in practical things and she loved to bake, a skill she had honed with Edie, so it wasn't long before she became a helpful addition to the Catering Team at The Falcon Hotel.

Considering how treacherous life was for other people in the country, their life was pretty good, with the exception of Frank not being at home, of course. Amelie even returned to writing articles and news for the local newspaper that she had once owned. It was only part-time work, but it was enough to keep them buoyant, along with RJs and Sarah-Lou's contributions into the family pot.

As the months and years of the second world war

rolled on, Frank found himself to be an important contributor to the war effort. He could not be spared by the RAF and so, like many other families, theirs had to endure long spells without their husband and father. Such was the life for most British families during the war. The only difference for their family was that they were relatively safe, living where they were. Having seen and listened to the news from London, so many others were not so lucky and the British people regularly mourned the deaths of far too many young men, whose lives had been lost, as well as those caught-up in the bombing raids.

Amelie kept herself informed of life in London and was shocked at the devastation reported there. Every day, she sent-up grateful thanks that her children were safe, as she hoped and prayed, they would never experience the terror of enemy bombs devastating their family life.

As the months rapidly flew by, Amelie continued to encourage her children to develop their own lives and in doing so, Ralph-James soon found himself a sweetheart. Much like Amelie and Caden had done, RJ and his sweetheart, Katie, also spent any free time they had down at the beach, walking, surfing, or even swimming in the new sea-pool whenever they could. For them, those snatched, precious moments together, made the war seem far away and they dared to dream of what the future might hold. Assuming they would survive the war.

Katie was a local girl whom Amelie warmed to immediately and she excitedly reported on the progress of RJ's romance in her many letters to Frank who, on hearing the first news, wrote back to say how much he looked forward to meeting young Katie when he was next home. Of course, that hoped-for visit, dragged on for several months before Frank was finally able to meet Katie. But, when the time came for his visit home, Frank made his way to Bude at the fastest possible pace and as his train reached the platform, the four of them were stood waiting, excited and overwhelmed at seeing him again. Their welcome home, took Frank's breath away and as he stepped down from the train, their love reached out to him, as arms embraced him and hugs, smiles, and kisses were shared. Those two days were so precious to them all and Frank was overjoyed to see for himself, just how well his family had adapted and settled into their new life. With all that had happened during the war so far, Frank's previous hesitations and concerns were banished in the blink of an eye, knowing a good future lay ahead for them all, once this thing was over.

Soon after returning to Brize Norton from his two-day pass, Frank was himself enrolled as an RAF pilot. Even though he was an American Engineer and officially on-loan, he was also a much-needed additional pilot and despite the abject fear of his family, within weeks, he too was flying off to join the war on the other side of the English Channel.

Amelie's stress levels grew weekly, along with every other wife and mother who had seen their precious loved ones depart to fight a war. The true horrors of which, none of them could ever imagine. As those weeks and months turned into years, they became the worst of Amelie's life and she feared the loss of another husband. It was a hard task to try and keep a positive outlook when the danger of losing Frank was so very real to them all.

The war had already taken its toll on the families in Bude and many sons, fathers and brothers had not returned. Every family feared receiving the telegram that would tell them another man was missing in action, or worst still, had been killed. Amelie was thankful that her own son, being American, was not called-up into the

British Forces.

RJ's secret intelligence work was supporting the war effort well and he felt extremely proud to be involved and doing his bit for his adopted country. A chip off the old block, his Grandpa Mike would have said, had he known anything about it. Of course, in truth, none of the family knew anything of the details of RJ's work, because true to his oath, he never spoke of it. In fact, for much of the time, even Amelie never knew exactly where he was and just assumed he and Katie were together whenever he wasn't working at the farm, which was his official cover story for any questions asked about what he did, or where he was.

Then, in 1944, the American's came to Bude to train for the D-Day landings. It was an exciting time for RJ because finally, in addition to his intelligence work, he felt able to support his fellow countrymen. It was also a very unsettling time, because RJ realised that many of the GI's he had come to know, would likely not return from France. The loss of life in this war was only too real and he was under no illusions as to the risks involved for his fellow countrymen.

The American Soldiers were billeted with local families, who welcomed them into their own homes, many wishing they were their own boys, whilst happy to help in whatever small way they could, hoping that someone would do the same for their young men.

The American Soldiers were thankful for the homely welcome they received from the people of Bude and to show their gratitude, often shared their field rations of candy, cigarettes and chewing gum. All of which became very popular among the younger towns-folk, with mutual exchanges becoming a regular activity.

Amelie found herself offering to billet two young

soldiers, one of whom, Jack Gill, very quickly became enamoured with Sarah-Lou and despite their young age, the two soon found themselves falling in love. Amelie could see the immediate attraction between Jack and her daughter, but she worried that Sarah-Lou's heart would be broken when the young GI returned to America, or worse, never returned at all from France. Sarah-Lou had her own ideas though and unwilling to accept the risk of Jack not returning from France, she secretly planned to return to America with him, once the war was over. Being young and fairly naïve, the pair had no idea when that would be, or if it was even possible, but like many others, the state of war made them less caring of obstacles and more determined to be together, no matter what. Such was the pressure of war-time relationships.

It was not long before Amelie realised her daughter's budding romance was very much more serious than she had hoped and Amelie realised in her heart of hearts, that once the war was over, she too would likely find herself in a similar situation to Edie and Mike; saying goodbye to one of their children. Expecting the worst, Amelie believed that the young couple would choose to return to the other side of the Atlantic Ocean. Whilst she reconciled herself to the idea by thinking of it in terms of karma, still she hoped against all hope that Sarah-Lou might choose to remain in Bude. Realising it was unlikely Jack Gill would be allowed to stay, meant the two of them leaving was an inevitable conclusion.

As the romance between Sarah-Lou and Jack blossomed, so did that of RJ and Katie, and before long, young Katie found herself to be pregnant. It was a shock to the two of them and to their respective families. Amelie had not expected to find herself becoming a grandmother quite so soon, particularly as the pair were not married, but sure enough, that was the very real and unexpected situation. Amelie wished Frank was there to support her, but he wasn't and as much as he would want to be, Frank was not going to be allowed home for a long time yet.

Naturally, and because Ralph-James was already madly in love with Katie, on finding out that their first love-making session had resulted in a baby being on the way, he did the honourable thing and proposed to her, promising to look after both Katie and their baby. RJ had loved Katie from the moment he laid eyes on her and whilst it had not been their plan to marry just yet, he was secretly excited at the prospect and hoped he would not disappoint her, or their parents.

With little money to splash out on a wedding, their marriage was simple but, being young, they were both full of hope for the future. Katie and RJ were over the moon at the thought of becoming parents, partly because each loved the other with a naivety that only the young experience and neither really thinking of the practicalities involved.

As expected, Frank was unable to join them for the wedding, due to the restrictions on all home-leave, but despite feeling extremely disappointed, knowing the current situation in Europe, RJ accepted his father's role was far more important at this crucial time.

Thankfully, Katie's family had been overjoyed at the news of a wedding and a grand-child, and their excitement had helped compensate for Frank's absence. RJ was very well thought of by his in-laws, who viewed him as the son they never had. It had not taken long for them to be as charmed by RJ as Katie had been and they had come to know him well. Ralph-James had impressed them immensely.

Frank wrote to the newly-weds, sending them his love and best wishes for a happy future together, adding that he hoped the war would end soon, so he could return home to join his rapidly expanding family.

Frank's treasured letter meant so much to Ralph-James, that he would keep it safe for the rest of his life.

Despite the months of intense training, the American's suffered extremely heavy losses at the D-Day landings and the family were fearful for both Frank and Jack's safety. So many young men had been killed, that both Sarah-Lou and Amelie feared the worst, whilst praying daily, for the best.

Thankfully, their prayers were answered when Jack Gill turned out to be one of the lucky ones. Yes, he was badly wounded, but he was alive. Relief washed over them all and they were happy, until they were informed that he was to be sent directly back home to America, bypassing any chance of returning to Bude. Sarah-Lou was beside herself with pent-up emotion, not knowing whether to be relieved, scared, worried or devastated. She again settled on relieved when, in a letter to Sarah-Lou, Jack advised her that due to his injuries, he *was* being sent back home, but he was also expected to make a full recovery. Jack had taken a bullet to his abdomen, which by some random miracle, had missed his vital organs, before ripping its way through his body and out of his back. So as not to worry her into thinking he would abandon her, Jack promised to send money as soon as he was able, so that Sarah-Lou could join him.

Already feeling relieved beyond words that Jack was alive and safe, albeit wounded, Sarah-Lou cried when she received his letter, which confirmed he loved her and still wanted a future with her. She was desperate to be with him and worried about how bad his injury truly was, suspecting he was making light of it to protect her. Not being a medical person, Sarah-Lou could not quite believe how Jack had even survived such an injury and knowing the war would keep them apart for a good while yet, the separation became an almost unbearable burden for her.

Jack's letter had also brought back painful memories for Amelie, remembering her own letter from the World War One trenches, when Dylan had lost his battle for life.

Now though, it seemed that her daughter was even more determined to join Jack and whilst Amelie found herself still hoping that Sarah-Lou would stay in Bude, her years of experience knew how strong young love could be, and how determined her daughter actually was. After all, wasn't that how she and Frank had raised her. Amelie resigned herself to the fact that Sarah-Lou would likely return to America, once Frank returned from the war.

It was true that Sarah-Lou was desperate to see Jack, but she also could not bear to leave without seeing her father one last time; realising there would be little chance of a reunion, once she had returned to America. It was a bitter-sweet decision to leave her family behind in England, whilst knowing she would be returning to her homeland and Jack, her own true love. Of course, her grandparents and the rest of the Carter family, made it a sweeter pill to swallow, but Sarah-Lou had found her choice overwhelmingly tough at times, yet she also knew she did not want to live without Jack.

Having kept Edie and Mike informed of all the family changes, Amelie was grateful to learn that Jack actually lived just fifty miles away from the Carter family, which meant Sarah-Lou would be able to see them regularly. That knowledge brought with it a huge sense of relief to Amelie and she told Edie as much in almost every letter she wrote. With all that said, Amelie's heart was also torn, not only had they left behind the Carter's and suffered the unbelievable wrench that had been, now they would be suffering again, when the time came to say goodbye to their beloved daughter.

But, before any of that could happen, Amelie needed Frank to come home.

As the months ticked by, Amelie and Frank wrote to each other regularly and before they knew it, the time had arrived for Amelie to tell him of the joyous news, that Katie had given birth to a son, their first grand-child, who was to be given the official name of Frank's own father, Michael, but whom they would all call Mikey. The whole family were touched by the chosen name and for Mike, in America, well, he felt like the proudest great-grandfather that walked the Earth. Frank was emotional when he read the news in Amelie's latest letter and wished more than ever to be back home with his family. This war had to end soon, surely.

Little Mikey was a healthy baby, who brought such joy to their family, that it felt as though the glue that had seemed to unravel soon after they had left America, was finally re-setting and new family-life bonds were growing ever stronger. Their new lives were now cemented in Bude and the future was beginning to look rosier than it had done for a very long time.

Once her little nephew had arrived, Sarah-Lou was tempted to stay in Bude, close to her mother and their growing family. Amelie had been their unbelievable tower of strength, a Mama whom they all greatly admired and respected for having lived the life that she had and how she always supported their every decision. But Sarah-Lou's longing for Jack soon returned, when his next letter landed on the doormat. Jack was ecstatic at the news that RJ and Katie had a son and told Sarah-Lou how he felt even more desperate to see her again. Jack wanted a family himself and he wanted Sarah-Lou to be the mother of his children. Explaining this in a letter, Jack also wrote to say he would be granted military accommodation once he was married, so, it seemed their future life was already mapped out and stable. Sarah-Lou was back in USA-bound mode, although, still desperate for her father to return home and to see him again, before leaving for her new future in America, with Jack.

It was a trying time for so many families as they longed for the end of the war, including those in Bude, who had also heard that many of the young GIs they had grown to truly care about, would never be able to return to their families. So many lives had been lost in the D-Day landings, that too many families lives would never be the same again, as British fathers, sons and brothers would also never return. Losing so many young lives was unbelievably sad and it felt like it would take a lifetime to recover from such terrible losses, no matter which side of the Atlantic the families were from. Many younger women who had been left with permanent memories of their GI love-affairs, caused more heartache. Amelie felt for them all. Many of those women had loved so briefly and then lost their young men forever. The fathers of their new-born children would never be returning home, having lost their lives on the Normandy beaches. Others, like Sarah-Lou, were lucky enough to be joining their sweethearts in America; once money could be saved for the journey they would have to make by sea.

When the last of the American troops had left Bude, life settled into a different routine, until finally, exactly six years and a day after the war first started, the new Prime Minister, Winston Churchill, made an announcement the whole country had been praying for... it was 2nd

September 1945 and the end of World War Two had finally arrived!

Such was the blessed relief to hear the news that the war was finally over, that when the announcement came, the whole population of Bude poured out onto the streets to celebrate. Some were stunned, whilst others were jubilant, but all were thankful that the war was finally over!

Many families grieved their personal losses, whilst others sent out thanks for the safe return of their young men, longing to see them again and knowing that day would be with them very soon.

Amelie and her family were amongst the celebrating crowd, when, whilst jumping up and down, hugging friends and crying tears of joy, a familiar voice called out her name, "Amelie!"

Turning in the direction of the voice, Amelie's heart skipped a beat as she saw the man battling through the crowds towards her, "Oh my goodness, is it you? Frank?" Amelie's heart filled with a joy like never before, as she pushed through the crowds towards him. Frank was home! He was safe! Her Frank was back!

As Frank reached Amelie, he wrapped his arms around her, picking her up and swinging her around before planting a passionate kiss, on the soft lips that he had been dreaming about. Those lips and that smile had kept him going through his darkest moments, and for a moment, they took his breath away. Holding Amelie away from him so he could look into her beautiful eyes, Frank grinned, before pulling her back into his arms once again and lifting her off her feet, swinging her around, again and again, not caring who saw them. Frank really didn't care because he was home and desperately falling in love with his wife all over again, and when his heart settled enough so that he could speak, Frank told Amelie that he loved her more than he could have ever imagined.

Amelie's own happiness was clear for everyone to see, as she told Frank that he was her hero, her most precious of people, her brave husband and that she loved him more than words could ever say. As Amelie and Frank held each other for the longest time, their hearts and minds exploded with a joy that filled their bodies like a rush of pure adrenalin.

Unable to wait any longer, Sarah-Lou rushed towards her father, quickly followed by Ralph-James. Hugging his crying daughter to him, Frank's arms reached out to pull RJ into him as well. Holding them tightly, his tears proved the love he felt, as he pulled them back to look into their faces and then hugged them to him again. As Amelie joined their family hug, neither she nor Frank wanted to ever let go, still not quite believing that they were all safe and well. As RJ stepped back, he ushered Katie and Mikey towards Frank, proudly introducing them to his father and not caring about the tears of happiness that were rolling down his face.

Later, as their family celebrated Frank's return, he proudly took great delight in officially welcoming Katie and little Mikey into their family. Because, he said, now that he was back, he wanted them to know how much he already loved them, from the letters that Amelie and RJ had written to him. There was so much to talk about and catch-up with, but Frank said, he and Amelie had some happy news they wanted to share and although he had been rehearsing this in his head for so long, he couldn't wait any longer and just blurted it out.

Explaining how both he and Amelie felt their future was in Bude from the first moment he and Amelie had walked along the beach, they had been making plans to settle permanently and watch their family grow. Now, sitting around the table and sharing their first meal together, Frank told them more about his and Amelie's ideas, explaining that whilst he had been gone, they had written to each other constantly, often talking about the options for their future and their family. Amelie explained that because of the risks of Frank being shot-down, they had agreed to wait until he returned home, safe and well, before they shared their plans with them. As everyone listened with baited breath, Frank explained that with Sarah-Lou returning to America to be with Jack – he smiled approvingly at his daughter, even though inside, his heart was breaking to know she was leaving – both he and Amelie wanted to set up a business, which would provide their family with some security and give them something they could all work at, together, to create a new and thriving future for them all. Which, he added, was no mean feat, considering the hard times of the recent war years. So, they had decided to purchase the small grocery store, on the corner of The Crescent, along with the two houses on either side of it. One of the houses was to be a new home for Ralph-James, Katie and little Mikey to live in, and the other was for him and Amelie to share. RJ and Katie were stunned, their very own home, what utterly unbelievable and exciting news!

Feeling excited, if not a little over-whelmed, this happy news was the future that Frank and Amelie had dreamed of, throughout the difficult war years. Both had wanted to support their growing family and offer them a future to build on and be a part of. Most families they knew had so very little and having lost their men-folk during the war, would definitely feel the harshness of a life without a regular wage coming in. Frank wanted their shop to serve their local community and offer a place where each person felt welcome to come along, and chat to each other, without feeling pressured into buying something on every visit.

Amelie joined in the excited chatter, explaining that she and Frank wanted their family to feel as though they truly belonged to the Bude community. Because, quite frankly, it was a miracle that they were all together and had survived the war, so, to have a safe home and a bright new future to work towards, together, as a family, their lives could begin to prosper again.

Hugging Sarah-Lou, both Amelie and Frank said she would be missed more than she could ever know, but they would send over money whenever they could, so she could visit them and bring Jack with her. As they wished her all the happiness in the world with Jack, Amelie and Frank hugged her to them as if they would never let her go again.

Sarah-Lou was filled with so much love for her parents and told them, that knowing she could come back to visit one day, just made the leaving part a tiny bit easier.

Frank held Sarah-Lou's hands in his and kissing them both, he told his daughter that she would always be his little girl and that no matter where in the world they were, they could look up at the same moon and know that their love could never be broken. Then, smiling at Amelie, his eyes twinkling, Frank hugged each member of his family again, before reaching for Amelie's hand. As he gently pulled her towards him, he placed her hand over his heart and full of emotion, Frank smiled at her and told Amelie how happy he was, but also, how very proud he was, of all she had achieved for their family, thanking her for keeping them safe and making him the happiest man in the world.

Frank was a man who was beyond proud to call Amelie

his wife and he promised he would love her until his dying breath, and then again, when their souls would eventually reunite in the spirit world. And with that, he kissed Amelie like she had never been kissed before… and as an immensely sensual love filled their hearts, their kiss finally released Caden's spirit back to the universe. Amelie was Frank's wife now and they would enjoy their forever future together.

The End

A few words from the Author

My final thanks go to you, my lovely reader, for taking the time to read this story, which was inspired by the family history of my friend's Mike and Joe, who now run The Crescent Post Office and Stores in Bude. This store is much-loved by the

Bude community and has been owned and managed by the Smith family since the 1930s.

I hope you have enjoyed this story and if you would like to read more written by me, there are three other books, each with very different storylines and characters. All are available online or via my own website, https://www.johannajackson.co.uk/books

	Working undercover, an MI5 agent is instructed to do whatever it takes to bring down the Mafia family he has infiltrated. As promises are made and broken, secrets lead to enforced lies and danger of death is ever present. Always the professional and keen not to blow the whole operation, the MI5 agent becomes embroiled in a situation which questions his principles, as drug-induced sexual experiences with the Don's daughter distract and challenge his loyalties. The question is, who will be hurt and who will survive?

Craving a calm, peaceful and uncomplicated life, through unexpected circumstances, Kellie finds herself living back in the same place she spent most of her childhood holidays. As her new life begins to settle, strange dreams start to invade Kellie's senses and she finds herself drawn to ancient Egypt. An old love triangle re-surfaces and previously untold stories emerge, which keep Kellie guessing as to what it all means. Sudden, tragic events cause the life she has come to know to take a dramatic turn and Kellie finds herself facing a different connection; one that links her present life, with one from a distant past.

Although shocked to find she has reached her thirties and is still unmarried, Casey enjoys her single life and the attentions of more than one man. With a good dose of raunchy fun and the complications that multiple men can bring, her life is certainly interesting. It is Casey's experiences of friendship, loss, lust and worries, along with her dreams, which she decides to share in an Online Diary. In doing so, she captures the interest of someone who is able to influence great change in Casey's life, just at a point when a serious issue interrupts her progress.

Book testimonials are available via this link -
https://www.johannajackson.co.uk/testimonials/